NORTH BY WEST

Two Stories from the Frontier

Books by R. D. Symons

NORTH BY WEST

WHERE THE WAGON LED

THE BROKEN SNARE

NORTH BY WEST

Two Stories from the Frontier

R. D. SYMONS

Doubleday Canada Limited, Toronto, Ontario
Doubleday & Company, Inc., Garden City, New York
1973

ISBN: 0-385-07475-1
Library of Congress Catalog Card Number 73-79717
Copyright © 1973 by R. D. Symons
Printed in the United States of America
First Edition

To the memory of
Arthur Symons

Contents

NORTH BY WEST

Two Stories from the Frontier

THE GARDEN
OF THE MANITOU

The Prophets described what they saw in visions as real. . . .
The Apostles the same; the clearer the organ the more dis-
tinct the object. A spirit and a vision are not, as the modern
philosophy supposes, a cloudy vapour, or a nothing. . . .
He who does not imagine . . . in stronger and better linea-
ments than his mortal eye can see, does not imagine at all.

WILLIAM BLAKE

PREFACE

Gardens are—or should be—places of peace, havens for quiet introspection. They are older than man, yet they follow man everywhere.

Gardens can be as small as a creepered bower or as large as the horizon.

They can be formal; bounded, close-knit, built, planted, and enclosed by the arts of man. Such gardens are the result of a nice discrimination in arrangement, of painstaking care in dressing, and they call for an intimate knowledge of grafting, training, and pruning no less than a fine craftsmanship in digging and sowing.

No less fine, no less peaceful, are the gardens sown by the Creator's hand. One such garden is the early Canadian prairie—the Garden of the Manitou. Here, amid herbage as many-hued and as intricately patterned as any Turkish carpet, orange lilies turned their faces to the sun, blue-eyed grass stared with the innocent gravity of a child, and wolf willow rippled in the moonlight like spilt quicksilver. Between the ranked poplars were open glades incarnadined with Indian paintbrush, while all around a million oval leaves danced and dipped and fluttered as the music of the birds and wind instructed them.

If you should ask me how I came to write this story, I must answer, "Because I had to." Kissikowasis—Morning Child—said I should.

It is not my story but a very old story of a very ancient people; a story which came to me through the lips of dark-skinned men who, perhaps because they had not been to school (as we know it), were still able to see what was born in the head and the heart.

I heard it in bits and pieces beside the Great Skeena River of British Columbia as the waters roared and frothed and the paddlers laughed through the cold spray; on the narrow mountain trails of the Chilcotin as Cedar Johnny and Charlie François talked together; in the skin lodges of the Dog-Ribs as the blizzard skidded across the muskegs, heightening the clipped Athabaskan tongue; by the flowing Saskatchewan as the prairie flowers danced to the lap of waters and the geese-people called from the sky; but mostly from the mouth of the last great Medicine Man of the Cree.

Myth, legend, and truth are intermingled here as they are in all history. Perhaps imagination and memory are closer to truth than we think.

Evolution, reincarnation, transmigration, and extrasensory perception are big words; but, as Morning Child would say, they are but words made up, not "born in the head," although they convey an old understanding. I think that simple words are best.

Mankind is very old and we are all children of our fathers and mothers; and if blue eyes or brown eyes are come by naturally, perhaps the same is true of our tag ends of thoughts and dreams. Only nothing can come from nothing, and what comes unbidden to the spirit of man must have had a beginning in truth.

Facts do not tell all.

Among the mountains and the waters and the forests and the prairies a story like this falls into place and seems not only natural and right but easily understood.

So the best place to read this is among the orchard trees, or in some quiet nook in a city park, down by the sheepfold, or by the flowing waterside where the fish-people make circles and the reeds huddle close, or in an old attic where you can see the great beams which once stood full-leafed in the forest. Or better still, if you live west of Winnipeg, read it on a grassy knoll when the first wild crocuses are in bloom and the wind plays with the pages as you turn them—and sometimes stop reading for a bit and just look, for the Garden of the Manitou will be spread before your eyes.

R.D.S.

Silton, Saskatchewan
June 1972

CHAPTER I

Morning Child

Morning Child was very old.

He was the last Medicine Man of the Kristinow people—the Cree. His hair was long and white, not braided but lying in locks over his shoulders. Around him was wrapped a tanned buffalo robe, very old, worn into wrinkles and glazed with willow smoke. It was covered with little pictures stained into the soft leather with berry juices.

Morning Child was also a friend of mine, so one day, full of curiosity, I ventured to ask him if he would tell me the story told on his robe. And the old Medicine Man spoke, and I have set it down. Not all at once, for sometimes he would fall asleep; but afterward he would wake, and I would fill his pipe, and he would speak on in the Cree tongue which laps against the ears like soft ripples of water, and sometimes he would pluck at his robe and touch a place with a lean forefinger to make a point and show a picture.

It was in the evening of a long-ago day when Morning Child began his story, and all around the frogs were peeping in the sloughs and the plovers were crying. And as we sat on the young grass I watched the Indian mothers nursing their babies and saw the little boys and girls laughing at their play.

In June we had heavy rains—for that is the month of rain—and we sat within the tepee of Morning Child, the tall painted tepee that was the last of the old kind on the Reserve.

Then came the Time of Grasshoppers, and now between the sentences we could hear them telling *their* old story, which is, I think, in a language long forgotten.

And when he showed me the Sign of the Two Rivers etched on his robe—the river that flowed south and the other that crawled north and east (each with a lake at its end)—I saw in my mind that these could only be the Great Rift Valley which goes from Lake Tanganyika in Africa to Lake Baikal in Siberia and I wondered; but I held my peace and spoke not, for it was his story.

When he spoke of the taiga, Morning Child said he did not know what that meant—it was a word only. And when he said, "Hear, O Israel" (but in Cree, *"Ayeehe Ishrayuk"*), I started and was suspicious. I asked him if he had learned that from the Black-Robes—the missionaries—and he thought awhile, his mild eyes peering from the wrinkles of his face into mine, and he said no. *"Numooya*—no!" like that. For, said he, man is very ancient, and why should not a saying be still in the head? (Born in the head, he said.) He was, he added, a priest and a diviner, a day-seer (not, like his father Stone-Gazer, a night-seer), and he said with some emphasis: "For I see these words behind my eyes, and when spoken they are sweet to the ear, like honey."

And when he spoke of the Narrow Sea of Salt I knew he meant the Strait of Bering, and by the Way beyond the Shining Mountains to the Pass of the River he meant the Rocky Mountain Trench and the rise of the waters of the Athabaska. But I said nothing.

And again when he spoke of the evil power of metal, I remembered that of old the Talmud was to be copied only by hand, for in the traditions of the Hebrews metal was symbolic of disunity and war. And again I said nothing.

And he began to speak in this way (for he was blind and did not know whether he was speaking to one or many):

"Listen, my chiefs and young men!

"Listen, my children . . ."

CHAPTER II

The Place of Tents

It was long, long ago (began Morning Child) that we, the people of the Kristinow, came from far in the west, from beyond the Shining Mountains where the eagles make their nests.

See! Here on my tanned robe are the marks! And here—see?— is the place we started from. It was a garden, a prairie set with trees and flowers. And here came a river gushing forth, divided in two branches, the one to the south, the other to the north and east.

And there was a strong man of the people who worked in metals of every kind to make a covering of scales like a snake's scales for the warriors, and who made swords and shields and all manner of things that can be beaten from metal. But metal causes disunity and trouble, and the Manitou (who holds the north and the south and the east and the west in the hollow of His hand), the great Manitou was displeased, and caused the earth to quake, and the valleys of the beautiful rivers were cracked and fissured and the waters disappeared.

The people were dispersed, some journeying to the south following the crack, and some to the north following the fissure which was in many places difficult to find since it ran beneath the earth.

And in the course of many generations, when these events had become dim, like pebbles beneath the water after the first ice has formed, there came to be a large camp of people northward from the Lake of the Last Fissure, and the land on which they camped and hunted was the Taiga. Do not ask me why. It is a name.

And of the people of the Taiga only the very old knew what

had been told by their grandfathers, but they did not keep silent, for they taught the people. All through the wanderings they had held to certain traditions. They knew only one God, who was a spirit. They made their camps in a certain way. They observed cleanliness and never suffered that water with which they washed the body to touch the face. They kept the right hand for food only. They braided their hair. And above all they did not let a widow (unless she was very old) remain husbandless, for it was right that the nearest of the dead husband's relatives should take her to wife—no matter though he had a wife already—so as to raise up children in the dead man's name.

In the Taiga there was game to kill, both for meat and for clothing. They killed animals with deadfalls and snares and pits, and sometimes with bows and arrows, for there was much flint from which to make cunning arrowheads and other artifacts of stone.

They had Shamans—which is a word—I think they were Men of Medicine; and they had feasts and ceremonies.

And so the years passed into forgotten ages, and then came Berry-Woman.

One day Berry-Woman left the camp, and on a slope of the Taiga, near the foot of a mountain, she began to pick berries which she intended to dry for winter.

As she stooped to her picking (for the shrubs were low), she heard a movement behind her in the brush but did not turn her head, only called out. For she thought it was another woman come to pick, and she was jealous of the berry patch she had found and had no intention of sharing it.

Then she felt a heavy hand on her shoulder and she turned her head. What she saw frightened her so badly that she could not scream, for it was a large Bear who had thus accosted her. She looked at the golden eyes and the brown muzzle and felt less afraid, for the Bear did not look unkindly at her. And she remembered that, after all living things had first come from the waters, it was the Bear who had first stood upright as a man does.

"My Lord Bear," she finally said, "I must hurry home, for

my brothers will be hungry, and I must cook a dish of meat with some of these berries for them."

But, while the Bear allowed her to rise, he would not permit her to return to the camp; rather, he seized hold of her skin garment with his teeth and led her up the mountain.

Some of her companions, picking berries at some distance, saw the Bear and the woman outlined on the top of a ridge, but only for a moment—then they both disappeared. The women found the upset berry basket and the tracks of the Bear but dared venture no farther, and on their return to the tents only said very simply: "Our sister has gone with a Bear." And the people said: "She shall be called Berry-Woman, for berries were her undoing."

Many, many years later, when most of those people were dead, a very old woman came down from the mountain to the tents. She was followed by seven sons, very tall, very powerful, very haughty and fierce-looking, and their faces were painted with the juice of berries.

The people were afraid (because of the haughty look of the sons) and remained in their tents.

Then the oldest Shaman came out and greeted the woman, asking whence she came and who she was.

The woman looked hard at the Shaman for a long time and then she spoke. "Do you not know me? I am she who went with a Bear."

The Shaman shook his head. "There *was* a woman who was put under a spell by a Bear. That woman is dead long since. The Bear took her to kill and devour. Today we kill every Bear we see in memory of that one, whom we called Berry-Woman."

The woman spoke again and said: "I am Berry-Woman. I was not killed. The Bear was a husband to me. I can say no more for now, for when I speak of my good husband I must mourn afresh, as a widow."

So the woman sat down on the ground among the tents, and let down her hair, and filled her hair with earth and twigs and dead leaves, and mourned for as long as it takes to boil water with hot stones.

And all the time the seven sons—very tall of stature, very haughty and very fierce—moved not at all but looked away over the treetops. For sons must not see a mother mourn.

And when she had made an end to her grief, Berry-Woman removed the earth from her hair, and braided her hair, and tied the braids and threw them over her head, so that they hung behind as is still the custom.

And she spoke and said to the Shaman: "You are the Night Owl, the magician. I remember when you were a lad. And *you* do not know about me, Berry-Woman?"

The Shaman put down his drum, and he took the owl's claws out of his fawnskin bag, and he took the seven pieces of ivory with the marks on them (which had come from the cold Taigas, from the tusks of the beast of the cold Taigas), and he took the goose-quill whistle from around his neck, and the other ornaments and magic things, and he placed them on the ground and arranged them, and looked at them for a long time. And very humbly (for he was afraid because of the haughtiness of the sons) he made his reply. "I cannot tell."

And the woman replied and said: "You cannot tell because you are deceived by the thing of metal which is in your pouch. Give it to me."

And the Shaman opened his pouch of snakeskin, the pouch all dappled and streaked, and reaching within, took out the amulet of yellow metal which had come from the west many generations before and gave it to the woman.

And the woman said: "Life is spirit. Only spirit has wisdom. This is not a thing of spirit, it came from the cold ground and is dead. But much looking on dead things brings witlessness, which is death of the spirit while the body lives. And see? I put this back in the cold earth. But *I* bring you discerning and understanding of all life—life of birds and of beasts, of trees and waters and vapors. And I bring my seven sons which I bore back yonder," and she pointed to the smoking mountain. "And my sons shall take wives among you and be the fathers of seven tribes of men."

Then the people came from their tents, for they understood that the sons were going to steal their daughters, and they gathered together, some with stones, and some with slings and with small stones, and they prepared to stone the woman and her sons.

But the sons stood as close as touching and looked over the treetops and did not answer, so that not one of the people dared to fling a stone at all.

And the woman said: "It must be as I say, and you are to let us go in peace; my sons and their wives and myself."

The Shaman also said: "Let them go."

Then with one voice the people said: "Why should we let them go? They are few. We are many. We should bind them and keep them as slaves!"

And the Shaman said: "Woman, why should you be let go? Speak and say!"

But the woman only said: "Because of my vision on the mountain yesterday; so hear me out if you will."

CHAPTER III

Berry-Woman and Her Sons

Morning Child made a sign for his pipe and smoked for a while before he went on with his tale. Then he placed his finger on his robe and said:

See here? This is the circle made by the people of the tents when they sat to hear about the dream of Berry-Woman.

And Berry-Woman said: "Kill me a dog." (For there were many dogs among the tents.) And when they had killed a dog she said: "Dress and cook the dog for me and my sons." And they did so.

Then Berry-Woman with her sons ate of the dog and were satisfied; and that is why we have the Feast of the Dog.

After that Berry-Woman told her tale:

"Yesterday I had a vision, and in my vision I saw a multitude of people—seven peoples. There were the people of the west who walked in the Sign of the Bear, with two legs and yet four legs more. There were the people of the south, whose robes were not of skin but of weaving, and their robes were yellow, to be a nation of diviners. And a people of the east who became five nations; and people of Mountains; and people of the New Taigas, dwelling among many trees; and people of the Impounded Waters; and people of a garden from which gushes forth a river. And I was to be the mother of these people but, being old, how can I have more children?

"And I thought of my seven sons, how they could not have children, since they are lacking wives. And I remembered the Place of Tents and how there must be many women; and that is why I came. So give seven young women for wives to my seven young men and we shall leave you in peace, and you shall prosper by reason of our prospering. And if you do not we shall not prosper, neither shall you prosper, for a stranger must not depart without a present. You know that is a thing of old."

Then the Shaman arose and he made a divination of numbers, and he spoke to the people and said: "By lots you shall choose seven maidens for the seven sons and let them depart in peace."

And the lots were drawn and the maidens were given as the Shaman said; but there was much sorrowing in the tents, for the people said: "We shall not see our young women again." (Yet the maidens themselves were not sorry; for the sons of Berry-Woman were indeed tall and handsome.)

Then Berry-Woman and her sons withdrew a little from the tents and made a camp for themselves. But after the first year Berry-Woman spoke to her sons and said: "Tonight each one of you must leave your tent and your wife and lie naked on the hills so that you may dream your dreams. For you do not yet know —neither do I know except in part—who shall go this way and who that. There is much land and there are many places. So do as I bid you, while I myself go apart a little way to consider."

So when the night was past and the light come again, the seven sons presented themselves to Berry-Woman, and the two eldest said: "We have dreamed our dreams. And you, Mother, have you seen anything?"

And the woman said: "Yes. I have dreamed. And I must go to the east many days, perhaps years. Who comes with me?"

Then the eldest replied: "Not me. For I dreamed I must go west but not south and walk in the Sign of the Bear forever, not upon my own feet forever, but upon four feet and not upon a dog. I know no more." (And I knew that he was the father of the Russians, the ancient Scythians who worked and fought on horseback.)

And the second son spoke and said: "Not me, Mother. For I dreamed of going south toward the sun, and I saw many people in robes of yellow and they were my sons and my sons' sons.

And they kept the Feast of the Dog forever and wrote with brushes of hair and made divinations. I know no more."

And the other five sons spoke each in turn from the first to the last, saying: "I come, Mother. I have dreamed no dream and by that I know I must journey according to your dream."

So the eldest son went to the west, and the second to the south; they and their wives and their gear, which was put upon the backs of dogs.

And year by year Berry-Woman and her five proud sons and the wives of her sons traveled farther and farther from the Place of Tents. They always traveled east and a little north in search of the garden and the river of the garden that Berry-Woman had seen in her dream.

And the land became more barren and the sons and the sons of the sons (for the people multiplied in due time) began to complain and speak bitterly, saying: "The wind is always cold, and there is little to eat but the fish in the streams."

However, they journeyed onward, and after two generations they arrived at a stretch of salt water and, beyond, much mist. And they heard the cries of the big fish of the salt water—those fish with shining pelts and loud voices.* And they killed many of these fish and camped and tanned the skins for boots and cloaks and ate the fat meat and were comforted, except that because of the vapors of fog they could not see the end of the waters.

Now Berry-Woman was old—so old that twenty men could only just compass her years with their fingers and toes. And she knew it was time to go to the Far Sandhills, by reason of a new vision she had received. And she called her people, who had grown to number many families, and spoke to them from her couch (for her limbs had failed her).

She spoke in a strange tongue, by reason of the Spirit:

"Hear, O Israel, the Lord God is the Kisā-Manitou, and the name came to me in the night of my last vision. And the Kisā-

---

* I think Morning Child must have meant seals.

Manitou is the master of life and the morning star which you see in the east."

And the diviners, the Shamans (the eldest and the youngest of the five sons who had followed the woman), interpreted her words to the people.

And Berry-Woman spoke again and said: "Follow the morning star, which is called *Wabun*—the Light—and go still to the east."

And the people said: "How can we go east, Mother, seeing there is salt water and much vapor and we cannot see the end thereof?"

After a little Berry-Woman spoke again, and now she said (for the Spirit was within her): "Do you doubt the Great Spirit? Now listen. There has been a flood of the waters, but the flood is daily abating, and will be impounded forever in five mighty lakes. Only be patient for a spell, and the vapors will rise and you shall see the day-sun again. And you will see a narrow place, and on the far side dry land. And without waiting longer you must now kill the dark fish which bark like dogs and make boats from their hides, and the boats shall be called *chemauns,* which means 'they carry us over the floods.' Be ready, and when you see the day-sun and the far shore, launch your *chemauns* at once and cross, and do not tarry on the bar shore but turn south. For there shall be a freezing of the waters and of the earth, and a cracking of the trees by reason of the frosts. Much snow will come, and if you tarry you will perish.

"But go south on this side of the Shining Mountains in a fissure you will see. And after a space of years you shall cross the mountains and travel east to the garden and the river where even now the Kisā-Manitou is preparing a place for you.

"And I do not know, for it has not been given to me, how you shall pass through the mountains; but when I am departed to the Land of Spirits take a hair from my head, O youngest Shaman, and make a bowl of clay and fill it with water and lay the hair therein, and cover it well with fish gut, and tie down the gut and bind it fast lest the water spill. And when you see the hair—and you must look at it daily—and when the hair stands upright in fear, then you must camp. And you must not leave the camp, for the mountains will smoke and the earth will tremble and groan. Only wait till the pall of dust settles, and you will follow a new fissure and walk through fear, not looking back or turning, for if you do that, the fear will root your feet and will turn you to stone.

"For the smoking and the trembling will make a way and a pass like a doorway through the mountains, and you shall reach the garden.

"And now I see my Lord Bear, and he is no longer like a Bear but for his brown eyes (for long ago he had an enchantment put on him). And his face shines."

So Berry-Woman left the tents of men; and her sons, very proud even in their age, encased her earthly form within great rocks, but first taking a hair from her head. And she slept in peace.

And Morning Child also fell asleep (but not the last sleep) and spoke no more that night.

CHAPTER IV

The Long Journey

And when Morning Child spoke again to continue his story it was the Month of Rains, and we sat by a fire of willow twigs in the painted tepee and the Medicine Man laid on the fire a braid of sweetgrass. The sweet-smelling smoke melted in with the vapor of the smoking woods and the smoking ponds, for the earth and the water were warm, but the rain was cool.

Listen (said Morning Child) and I shall tell what befell the children of Berry-Woman after they had passed over the salt water. Then they left the *chemauns* and packed their goods upon their dogs and journeyed south. And they came to where they saw the Shining Mountains to their left hand; and there were mountains also on the right hand. They suffered hunger from scarcity of game and even worse hardship, for the cold became more bitter each night, and snow fell constantly. Year by year the snow and the cold increased, and they followed the tracks of beasts—for many beasts of all kinds also walked south, before the cold. But the beasts traveled fast and few fell to their arrows.

And in time the eldest Shaman died. But the younger Shaman lived, and it was he who carried the Medicine Bowl of the Woman's Hair, who was called Kristinow, the Cree. He was the seventh and now the last son, and he carried the Bowl.

But many of the people yearned to go west again, for they longed for the old places and lost their faith, doubting that the Garden of the Manitou did lie ahead. When they saw an easy pass through the mountains on the right hand they said: "Let us go to where we shall kill the great fish of the salt-chuck and be fat again, with shining faces!" And they held a council and the greater number, having much faith in Berry-Woman's vision, determined to press on in spite of the great difficulties and hardship.

But the discontented ones were allowed to depart, and I think they are there yet. I have been told that it is they who carve the images of the Bear and of Berry-Woman to this day, together with all manner of totems and images of ravens and of fish.

But the Kristinow do not carve, for the youngest of the old Shamans had said: "Grave no image of any living thing, only with the juice of berries draw the pictures for a reminder."

So the people of Berry-Woman led by Kristinow with the bowl traveled onward, and they left the Place of Great Cold behind them and the land became more kindly. For the space of many years they journeyed, always with the Shining Mountains on their left hand. Sometimes they camped for a year or more in the Valley of the Great Fissure, for the fish were fat in the river and sometimes there were deer, but not always. And they saw many shaggy bears, but these they saluted and went past by another way, doing them no hurt nor receiving any. For by passing by on the other side the people pleased the bears, who stood upright to watch with the juice of berries red upon their chops. And the mountains belonged to the bears.

Now the tongue of the people began to change a little, for there were new places to name, new animals and fish and trees to be named. Yet the chief Shaman and his young men who would be Shamans in time remembered and memorized many of the old words. That has continued, and that is why a day-seer like myself —Morning Child—may use a word which is a remembered word, so that you see fit to question me and ask: "From whom got you that word?" Truly, such things are born in the brain. They are behind the eyes.

And because the pine trees were tall and slim in this place, the tents became larger, not low as in the Taiga where for support there were but crooked birches. And this was better too, for the Old Ones have told that in the cold places, while they journeyed, the people had to dig dens in the ground like the dens of the shaggy bears which stood upright on the mountainsides to watch the people pass.

But still the mountains—very tall, very proud, like the sons of Berry-Woman in their youth—stood upon the left side looking over and above the treetops in their fierce pride.

And there came a sickness of age on the youngest son, the youngest of seven, who was called Kristinow. So the people camped below the rim of a great mountain whose top pierced the very clouds so that its greatest height could not be seen.

And the people brought a broth of goat's flesh to the seventh son, their chief Shaman, and when he had eaten he was somewhat refreshed. Then he spoke to the bearer of his medicine bundle (and he too was a Shaman, but untried) and said: "Bring me the Medicine Bowl," as he had done nightly.

And he gazed into the Medicine Bowl, and lo! the hair from the head of Berry-Woman stood upright in fright. (And nearly two generations had passed since Berry-Woman had departed to the Land of Spirits; yet still virtue was in her hair.)

Now Kristinow, the chief Shaman, gathered his pupils about him and said: "Warn the people. They are to eat and drink, and then to sleep on their bellies, not looking up, between the rocks, until a time is passed."

So the younger Shamans beat on their drums and blew on their goose-quill whistles and assembled the people, telling them of all that the chief Shaman had said. And the hair of the people stood up in fear, just like the hair from the head of Berry-Woman. And they lay down after eating, each with his wife and little ones, among the rocks.

It grew very dark and a wind arose and many trees fell, but the people were among the large rocks and suffered no hurt.

And the ground began to quake, and there was much smoke from the mountain, with groanings and lamentations of the earth. So the people put their hands over their ears; and each man pressed close each to his wife, with the little ones between them.

So the quaking continued, with bolts of lightning, and they heard the wings of a great bird beating overhead, so loudly that the people did not hear the beating of their hearts. And the spirit of Kristinow rested easily between his ribs, for he knew this to be no other than the thunder bird, which is loved by the Kisā-Manitou and by men, for the deadly rays from his eyes will never be directed toward a man of the Spirit. Nevertheless, the bird can divide mountains; for the strength of mountains lies in their pride and not in Spirit, seeing there is much metal within them.

I cannot tell you how many days this continued, for it was not told me. Nevertheless, the darkness turned to light, the wind abated, the ground left off from quaking and the smoke and the dust dispersed a little, and so the people began to come forth. They were covered with ashes, and they were very thirsty (for fear makes the mouth dry).

And they saw a shining place, a spring, a new spring where before the ground had been dry. And the people slaked their thirst and ate some dried fish. Afterward they saw that a small stream issued from the spring, and it ran eastward. So they packed their gear and left that place, following the stream.

And as they traveled to the east the vapors and the dust dispersed and the people saw that the mountain had been rent and a great fissure had appeared. But fear was upon them, for the two faces of the fissure were dark as if with rage, and great rocks fell from time to time.

And the people began to turn back, but Kristinow, the youngest son of Berry-Woman and the oldest of the Shamans, held up his hand to stay them and spoke and said: "Did not Berry-Woman say to walk through fear by the Spirit? How else will you hope to come to the garden and the river—the place which has been prepared for you?"

And an eagle screamed and flew eastward over above the fissure, turning neither to the right hand nor the left, and Kristinow said: "Follow the bird, for it is a sign. And turn not again, not a single one of you, or there shall be mourning in our tents."

So the people overcame their fear. Yet there was one who turned, for he had seen the glint of yellow metal in the stream by his feet. And he stands there to this day, in the likeness of stone, very burnished. And there was mourning for him in the tents.

After many days the fissure began to widen, the rocks ceased to fall, the stream became a river, and the people saw to the east, over the treetops of the great forest, a land on which the sun shone, and they took heart.

But that night, with the cruel mountains behind them, the wise Shaman Kristinow passed to the realms beyond to join the spirit of his mother Berry-Woman and his father the Great Bear of the Taiga. Before he died he buried the bowl deep in the earth.

And to this day the fissure through which the people passed is called in our tongue the Pass of the Hair, and sometimes the Place of the Man of Yellow Metal. But there has come confusion with time, and some now say the hair was yellow. But I do not believe this, for Berry-Woman was stricken with many years, and even in age our hair is dark. But what does it matter?

And now it is time for me to rest and commune with the Spirit, for I am tired with much remembering.

Tomorrow, in the evening, I shall tell you more; but for now, leave me.

And with these words Morning Child turned away his face, and I left softly, full of wonder that such a tale should have come down through so many years and so many people.

CHAPTER V

The World of Weesahkahchak

It was many days before I went again to the tepee of Morning Child. In the meantime I had written down, translating his words as best I could, all that he had told me.

And then, in the soft dusk, with grasshoppers whispering all about, I sat again in the familiar place and waited quietly while the old Medicine Man smoked the pipe I filled for him.

Outside two Indian horses cropped the grass side by side. In front of the next tent a man was making a small bow for his little boy. A woman was tanning a hide in the bushes, and I could hear the sweep, sweep of her shaving tool. The sweet smell of willow smoke filled the air, and it was as if we were living long ago, before the land knew the fumes of gasoline and the shuddering of trucks on gravel roads.

And then Morning Child laid down his pipe and took his two fans of eagle wings and held them crossed as he continued his story; for it was a medicine story.

And he spoke like this:

Listen! I have told you of Berry-Woman and her son Kristinow, and how they passed through waters and mountains.

Now you must know that, many generations before, at the time of the vision of Berry-Woman, the Kisā-Manitou, the Great Spirit, had already sent Weesahkahchak (whom he loved) to the land on this side of the mountains. And Weesahkahchak came, singing, in a great canoe of birch bark; for at that time there was no dry land. There was only water. The water took the great canoe and dealt gently with it, and it did not roll or heave. For in the canoe were also the firsts of the place-to-be.

There were the first deer and the first wolf and the first heron and the first beaver—there was the first of every creature that walks or swims or crawls or flies.

And they came to a place of the waters where all was placid and gentle, and the Manitou sent the beams of his sun to cast a light and a reflection on the waters.

And Weesahkahchak said: "This is a holy place and a kindly place. I shall make a world. And I shall also make living a people, that they may enjoy the firsts of the earth, and that there may be councils and wisdom and love, and children at play, and a laughing and a singing among the children of man.

"All things shall be good here, and the spirit of one shall speak to the spirit of another—only metal shall be hidden deep in the dark, for with metal comes confusion."

And Weesahkahchak bade the first muskrat dive and find some mud. So the muskrat came back with mud in his little paws, and Weesahkahchak said, "It is good." And he blew three times on the mud until it increased to great size, so that the canoe was on dry land, of which the end could not be seen, leaving only one pool of water. All the rest was dry land, and this was the place for the firsts of the new land.

Then Weesahkahchak drew on the soft land with his fingers and bade the pool of water run in the furrow he made, and called it Swift Sliding Current.

Weesahkahchak went south and made a high plain, and he went north and made a great forest, the Strong Woods. But in between he left everything flat, and he covered it with grass as a carpet and a lawn, and in parts he planted groves of poplar trees.

And he took the first antelope and spoke and said, "Your name is *apisicheakoos,* and you will live on the high plain and eat sagebrush."

And to keep the antelope company he sent the first bobcat and spoke and said, "Your name is *pah-pah-keo-pisoo* because you are spotted."

He also sent eagles, and many small birds and animals that as yet he had not time to name.

Then Weesahkahchak took the first moose and spoke and said, "You are *mooswa,* the Big Lip. Go live in the forest and the swamps and the willowland of the Strong Woods, for you may browse on twigs and eat the water plants. It is good."

And the first moose went, and for company he had with him many creatures. He had *kwochas,* the chattering squirrels, to warn him of danger and to throw down the spruce cones to make more trees. He had the woodpeckers to tap their drums in the Moon of Snows, lest it be thought the forest was too silent. He had with him the warblers to sing in the glades in the Moon of New Leaves, otters to play in the rivers, whitefish to swim in the lakes, and many more creatures to move among the great trees and the graceful ferns which had been planted there.

Then Weesahkahchak looked at the flat land between—the great flat land between the River of the East and the great Shining Mountains to the west; the great flat land whose south side laps against the sandstone buttes of the high plain and whose northern side touches the green fringe on the skirts of the Strong Woods. Weesahkahchak looked for long and long and then he said, "This shall be a prairie and a grassland and a pasture. This shall be the Garden of the Manitou. It is good."

And Weesahkahchak went to the bison, the great shaggy *mustus.* He spoke and he said, "Look and see that it is good; you shall rule everything in this land but the people who will come; for this land shall be the land of the youngest son of those-to-come, and they shall be the Kristinow.

"Go and measure it, foot by foot, yard by yard, mile by mile, year by year. Fatten on the grasses, shelter against the storms in the forested hollows and coulees and ravines of the Rapid Flowing River for always and forever. When the flies torment you, use your horns and your hoofs and dig a wallow that you may cover yourself with dust. When the warm winds of spring make you itchy under your winter hair, see?—there are great rocks upon which you may rub.

"Tread out the land. Pace it. Possess it. Let your bellows echo across from limit to limit. And when you die your bones will remain white among the grasses and be a memorial to you. Only, treat the grass with care, for it was a first; when you have grazed a day and a night, move on, lest the grass be wearied. It is good."

And the first bison trod his heavy way to his own. And for company he had the most beautiful of birds, the meadow lark, as well as a multitude of other favored creatures which Weesahkahchak had no time to name. There was *mist'shaganis,* the coyote, to warn him of danger. There were the great white cranes that stood almost as high as a man. And there were the geese-folk—the *neskuk*—to tell each year of the coming of spring.

Before he left, Weesahkahchak, who had a merry spirit, heaped up a great mound, and found that from its top he could see over mile upon mile of the Garden of the Manitou. Then he laughed, and, full of glee, he slid down from top to bottom, making deep grooves with his heels to break his speed. And by the Swift Sliding River which is called the Saskatchewan the hill stands to this day, and is called *Weesahkahchak-o-Saskatchewanik*—His Sliding Place. Then Weesahkahchak filled his pipe with sweetgrass and spoke and said, patting the ground, "This shall be called the Earth Mother"; and he saluted the Mother with three puffs of smoke.

Again he thought for a spell and then he spoke and said, "The Manitou, the Great Spirit, the Master of Life, shall be called the Father. And I think the Father shall love the Mother, and the Mother shall forever smile upward into the face of the Father. It is good." And he puffed three puffs to the Father and watched them dissolve in the blue above.

Then he departed into the realms of *peachim* and *tipiscow peachim,* which are beyond the last limits, and where abides the tepee of the Kisā-Manitou, the Great Spirit, the Master of Life.

So it happened, as the Old Ones still tell it; and if you do not believe them, go to the *o-Saskatchewanik,* and from the top look north, and you will see the banks of the Great River and you will know they are wooded, for the tops of spruce trees peep above the bank; look west and you will see the Eagle Mountains, and, beyond, the prairie plain, and in spring and fall the cranes will fly overhead and call to their lord the bison. But there will be no answer, for reasons I shall recount to you.

And if you listen at night from *o-Saskatchewanik* you will hear the lament of *mist'shaganis,* the little prairie wolf, for he still runs and stops and listens and runs again, seeking his lord the bison, in vain.

After that go out on the plain. Let your feet take you to the south, and you will see the hollows in the grass where once the lord of the plains made his wallows and covered himself with dust; you will see also great rocks all smooth and polished, for here he rubbed away his itchiness.

And many other creatures of the old days are here too, but they are not always easy to find. For metal brought fear to them, and they hide and tremble and always seek to escape when they hear footsteps on their prairie.

And now I must tell you that long after Weesahkahchak departed, but still long before the earliest memory of the garden, men and women came to the garden. They saw that everything was good in the garden and they said, "Surely this must be the place of the vision of Berry-Woman, so here at last we shall live always," for they were the very people who called themselves the Kristinow, the sons and daughters of Berry-Woman; who had passed through fear and who had traveled for so many weary generations and suffered such great hardship.

Their skin was the color of a hazelnut. Their hair was black and glossy, and their eyes were dark pools of happiness. The men were lean and hardy and the women were dainty but strong, with teeth as white as little shells. As for their children, they were plump and merry. People had called them the Smiling Ones in the land that knew them before. The language of the Kristinow was soft and musical, never raised in unseemly argument, and it sounded like the water running in the Great Swift River.

And when they had finished the store of food they had brought with them to the garden, they hungered and wanted meat. Then their Old Ones stood and spoke and said:

"O Brothers and Warriors and Sisters and Little Ones, hear us.

"It was long ago that Berry-Woman brought us to life, and a Bear was our great-great-grandfather very long ago. Therefore, kill the Bear only when you need fat, and deal honorably, not forgetting to say, 'Brother, I need you,' when you loose your arrows.

"Likewise the bison. He is lord of all on the prairie, save for us. Take him only when you need him. Moreover no man must take the bison by himself or for himself; only when the whole tribe decides and the priests have made medicine shall he be hunted. And his skull you shall leave on the prairie; do you not know that each night the Manitou must make a list, that he may bring to life again every creature in the Great Sandhills of Wapahki in the hereafter?

"*Amisk,* too, is king of the beaver-folk. His meat is good if meat ye must have, but do not throw his meat or his feet or his entrails to dogs; for is he not a king and the son of a king? The streams belong to the beaver, and his remains must go back to his own.

"Likewise the muskrat. The little white tip on his tail is a counter for the eye of the Manitou when he makes his accounting, and the Manitou does not look for *wuchusk* on dry land but in the water. So throw each tail tip there.

"And above all—you shall share and share alike in all meat. If a hunter kill a bison he is to share it with those who perhaps were not lucky that day. The sick and the weak are to be fed first. The land is the Manitou's as we and all flesh are the Manitou's. And now let us name all things. We have spoken."

And so the Old Ones named the birds and the animals, and they adjured the people to give them respect as brothers and sisters of men.

They gave names to everything that walked and ran and trotted and climbed and flew and swam. The rabbit they called *wapoos* because he is so white in winter. The elk they named *wabutek* because in the dark forest he too looked white. The bittern they called *mokasoo* by reason of his voice in the nighttime when he booms in the reeds.

The willow tree they called *neepeeya* and the leaves *neepeeseeya,* and because spring is the time of leaves they called that season the Moon of *Neepin.* The chickadee they called *puch'geeskees,* and sometimes spring bird because he calls *nee-pin* on warm days in March.

The shining stars they called *wesukwachuk* because they dance and twinkle, and they are sister worlds.

All the birds they called *peasis* if they were small, while the bigger ones were called *peaso.* The biggest of all, which sometimes threw a great shadow on the grasslands, they called the great *peaso,* the thunder bird, for it darkened the sky and brought hail and rain and lightning and thunder; but it was good, for it caught up the great serpents at its feet—the serpents that are cold and sleep in deep holes next to metal—and bore them aloft and away (for it was a serpent that first showed the man-of-metal that which is not good).

The deer-people gave them good skins to tan for leggings and cloaks, and the bison-folk gave them warm robes as well as meat, and the Kristinow-folk also made great tepees from the hides. They painted these tepees. They painted the Earth Mother around the bottom, almost black, using charcoal and goose fat. At the top they showed the *kissikow peachim,* the great sun, in all his splendor, using the red and yellow earth from the creek banks. And in between, very cunningly, they painted the representation of their medicine spirits as they had seen them in visions. Coyotes and bears and bison and wildcats, and many things too hard for anyone to understand now, all painted with red earth or the juices of berries and plants.

The stones they called *asini,* and they were earth friends, because they let themselves be chipped for arrowheads and knives and such things.

But in all the Garden of the Manitou they used no metal. The Old Ones always told the people that metal was a medicine for evil. Metal was cold. Metal did not receive the rays of the sun like grass and trees and stones and water. Metal alone did not have Spirit and It could numb the heart of man and close his ears. One metal was yellow and it was the chief of the metals; it was not good even to name that one. "Let us," said the Old Ones, "call all these things *pewabskwis* and never touch them." And they never touched them.

And the people were told to leave their hair long and make it glossy with the fat of *muskwa* the bear, in memory of the fact that the bear was once a man. And they were taught that to cut the hair was wrong, because without their braids the Manitou would not know them; but the hair on their faces was to be plucked out for cleanliness' sake.

And they were told to be merciful and not to pursue an enemy after he ran for safety; and that it was a greater honor and a more worthy coup to touch an enemy with the wood of a bow or the shaft of a lance than to spill his blood on the grass.

And so the people prospered and were happy. They moved their tepees to the grassland in summer and cooked by the heat of buffalo chips.

In winter they moved into the little forests that grew in the ravines and along the riverbanks, where their earth friends— *wabi-meetoos* the white poplar, *neepeeya* the willow, and *waskwei* the paper birch—gave kindling and firewood. Some indeed went north to the Strong Woods where they had friends, the Muskegoes, the Swampy People. There they hunted the moose, saving the hides to tan when spring came; and their earth friends, the pine and the spruce, kept them warm.

And in the Moon of Great Cold the Old Ones whose time had come put out their hands to *keewadin,* the northwest wind, who stopped their pain with his cool breath and took them to the Sandhills of Wahpaki, where their limbs would be young again and their eyes clear. And their relatives would mourn awhile, which is seemly. But afterward they would make an end to sorrow and wash their faces and take comfort as the *kissikow peachim* came higher overhead and melted the snow, and their sky brothers the geese flew over like great arrowheads out of the south, calling down to the earth folk that spring was here once more.

And those who needed new *chemauns*—brand-new canoes— went to the forest with their wives, and the wife chose the birch tree, for the birch tree is a woman too. And the husband made his cut right from top to bottom, and the birch tree gave her bark in one great piece, only weeping a little from the cut. But the wife said: "See, woman, I catch your tears in a bowl, and they shall be boiled and made sweet, and I shall drink them as a bond between us; a bond and a promise that I shall show the canoe to the Manitou, that you may burst out in new leaf in the Sandhills. It is good."

And the women and men then took the gum of the spruce tree, *minahik,* and the roots of the tamarack, *wakanogun,* and sewed and caulked and made a *chemaun* with which to follow the shining creeks, and to set their nets for *wabi-kinosao,* the sweet-fleshed whitefish with the jeweled eyes.

With the spring the land was filled with the singing of birds, the crying of the curlews and the peeping of the frogs from all the ponds that shone like mirrors. The grass grew green and the prairie roses blossomed far and wide, pink and sweet and fragrant, promising red fruit for the autumn for the women to mix with the berries of saskatoons and raspberries and the tiny prairie strawberries.

The skies were blue and the clouds were white by day but pink at evening. The grasses nodded and sang in the wind that went over them like waves. The harebells and the prairie flax pushed shoulder to shoulder and gossiped quietly, the way flowers do.

Pipits sang in the sky, redwings in the reeds, and robins in the poplars. The silvery wolf willow blossomed in tiny yellow flowers that made the whole prairie sweet, while in their clumps the catbirds and yellow warblers built their clever nests.

The orioles hung their cradles from the cottonwood trees that grew in the Valley of the Great River, and flashed like bits of sunshine from tree to tree.

In the Moon of Flowers you could sometimes see the dark

herds through the shimmer of the heat waves that danced and leaped like fawns over the prairie; and with the herds could be seen the buffalo birds, whose duty it was to follow the grazing beasts for mile upon mile and destroy the stinging flies dozing on the humps of the big bulls. The brown-feathered wives had no time to nest or they would have been left behind; instead they put their eggs in the nests of the little grass birds. But these little birds were good-natured, and they fed the foundlings with as much love as their own. All this the people knew had been ordained by the Manitou, the Great Spirit, the Master of Life.

Generations went by. Babies were born, grew up, married and had babies of their own; but still no metal came near the people of the Kristinow, and the children played among the earth friends without fear.

So the grass grew where it had been planted, the forest stayed in its place, the birds nested as had been ordained. The bison and the elk and the fox stayed where they belonged. The rivers ran the courses allotted to them. And for heat there was wood; for thirst water; for hunger meat; for covering there were soft skins; for man there was woman, and for children there was home.

For light there was *peachim*, the sun, and *tipiscow peachim*, the moon; but when the latter went monthly to her rest there was the Light-in-the-North that swept back and forth so that darkness might not be too dark.

And the Old Ones said, "It is good."

And now, said Morning Child, you must let me sleep. I have more to tell, but it must wait for I should think and choose my words with care, for there is something bitter to my mouth in telling you of what came to pass in later days.

CHAPTER VI

The People of the Garden

Again Morning Child was speaking. He said: Before I speak of the latter days I think it would be well to tell you how the Kristinow lived before the peace of the garden passed away. My people became great hunters. But they also had to be warriors, for the other tribes of the sons of Berry-Woman sometimes invaded their hunting grounds and had to be driven back. It had always been thus, even on the Taiga, even by the two great rivers. And by fighting and hunting the people kept their strength.

When they hunted the bison all the people went out and built cairns in diverging lines spreading outward from the top of a cliff or a cutbank. When the bison were driven, they kept between the lines; for behind each pile of stones there squatted a man—or perhaps a woman—who by suddenly standing up frightened the beasts so that they turned neither to the right hand nor to the left but kept straight on, galloping furiously so that they could hardly be seen for dust, and flung themselves headlong over the cliff so that many were killed.

Then the women of the Cree would put up the camp and go to the skinning and cutting up of the meat. The fat meat of the hump and the big blue tongues would be set aside for a feast, but the rest of the meat would first be diced and then ground between stones. Then it was mixed with sun-dried berries and fat—a great deal of fat—and was pressed into bags of bison hide and sewed up to be eaten in winter. This meat was called pemmican because it had much fat, and *pimiwokan* means a kind of fat.

And there would be many robes to tan. They were tanned in this way: First the hide was stretched flat on the ground and pegged down at the edges with pegs of saskatoon (for that shrub grows in every coulee); but when they were far from a coulee it was held down with stones. Then the flesh side was scraped with a bone scraper and much fat and brains worked in, and the robe thinned with the scraper till it was as soft as the breast of a wild goose.

But if a woman wished to tan hides for a tepee, then she threw the hide in a creek or a slough for about ten days. This caused the hair to loosen, so it could all be pulled out or scraped off, and this made good hides for a tepee. To make a big tepee took fourteen hides or even more.

The people kept many dogs. They knew they had always had dogs since they went to the Taiga, and these were still like the dogs of the Taiga. They were for eating at feasts as well as for carrying packs or pulling a *travois*. The dog *travois* was a pair of light poles fastened on either side of the beast, like shafts. The ends dragged on the ground, for the people knew nothing of wheels. These two shafts were joined by crossbars behind the dog, and between the crossbars was a rawhide lacework which served to carry bundles.

The women did most of the household work, and besides cooking and sewing hide garments they cared for the dogs, and what those beasts could not carry the women carried. For the tents were moved at least twice in every moon, because the game animals did not stay long in one place.

The men could not help the women, because they had to scout out the country ahead and see that it was free of enemies. If they did find enemies they had to drive them off so that their women and children would be safe.

The older boys sometimes went with the men, but the younger ones stayed with the women. Since a busy woman's hands must be always free, the babies were carried in a pouch on their mothers' backs and were able to look over the waving grass or up at the blue sky and then be lulled to sleep by the mothers' swinging walk. When the little ones became wet the mothers put fresh moss in the bags.

All things required for life were at hand. They had only to be looked for and taken.

If the camp was on a plain so windy that the force of the gale lifted the skirts of the lodge, then stones were at hand to hold down the hides round about. In the forest tree trunks or wooden pegs would serve, and in the sandhills—where stones are scarce— they could bury the tent skirts under the heavy sand.

There was water, which has a multitude of uses; and there was grass which could be plaited into a rope; and there were shrubs and small trees for arrows and for bows; there was sinew of bison for cords and for sewing; flint and other stones were not hard for the arrowhead makers to find.

And no one increased his wealth with these things, for all were free and put there by the hand of the Kisā-Manitou.

Now, after many people had grown up and died and many more people had done the same, there came to the Kristinow horses. And these horses they got first by stealth from the Crows (who are handsome people), and the Crows from the Pawnees, and the Pawnees from the very wild people who descended also from another of the sons of Berry-Woman and are called Comanches.

It was thought that the Comanches made these horses, but in truth the people were to find later that the horse had a master before the Comanches knew about them at all. The people were to learn this to their sorrow.

When the Kristinow first got their horses they were a little afraid, for horses are tall and bony beasts. But they found that the beasts could be tamed with ropes of rawhide. So another task fell to the women, in which they soon became skilled. A bison hide had to be cut in a long strip, starting at the outside and cutting to the center. And the women would braid four or more of the strips into a rope, making it pliable by passing it through a hole in a stick, after which it was stretched from tree to tree. Then two women, one on each side, would take the stick in their hands and push it the full length of the rope. This they did many times, bearing down hard upon the stick. Also they used a great deal of fat to rub into the rope. And a big heavy woman would be known as a good ropemaker by reason of the weight which she bore against the stick.

The young men soon became skilled in the use of these ropes for catching horses as well as for controlling them.

The hunters, by riding the fleetest of these horses, could now approach close to the bison and kill them with their lances and arrows, while the women on the more gentle and less speedy ones could follow with the camp gear. For now they made a *travois* for horses on which they could carry large loads and the children also, while the women rode upon them.

The women worked many cunning designs on the leggings of buckskin and the hunting shirts and the bison-hide shields of the warriors. For this they used bits of shiny river clamshell and the quills of porcupine dyed in bright colors.

When a man returned from hunting his wife would take off his trail moccasins (which had soles of bison hide, to protect him against the cactus spines) and replace them with a soft clean pair of lighter make. By custom she always fed her man first, and afterward herself and her children; for *they* could eat at any hour, but it was the man who traveled many miles on the hunt to find game, and when he returned he was hungry.

The Kristinow did not forget the Kisā-Manitou, the Master of Life, and they walked in the ways they had been told. The wise Men of Medicine did not allow them to forget. And at the sun dance, when the young men, having fasted and received their visions, had been adopted by their medicine spirits and become braves, then they all prayed to the Manitou.

For the Medicine Men said: "Great chiefs and brothers and people of the Kristinow, hear ye . . ." And it was as it had been in the far-off days when Berry-Woman said: *"Ayeetu Ishrayuk!"*

For all kinds of divination, and for healing sickness, and for wisdom and kindness, the Men of Medicine (which is understanding of holy things) were held in respect and reverence. What they could not explain they, in their wisdom, left alone, lest the people be confused.

And the people did not think too much of the morrow, for,

said they: "Shall we see another sunrise? Are not all things in the hand of the Master of Life? Should we fret and beat our robes at night for fear of our common lot? *Tapwā,* sleep is better."

So they lived in peace, no man plotting against his neighbor; only sometimes planning how to outwit the other tribes, for that was to protect them all, not any man for himself.

From time to time, when a quarrel with another tribe arose, a man was killed in battle; or a woman died in childbirth or because of sickness. This, they knew, was the common lot of all birds and beasts as well as men.

A dead warrior had his horse killed under the scaffold where he himself lay wrapped in his robe, for a man must be mounted in the Sandhills. *Kinikinik* (which was smoked like tobacco) and food and weapons were put by his side. The reason for putting the body on a scaffold was so that wolves would not disturb it; but if poles were scarce, the dead had to be buried in the ground and many rocks piled up for the same purpose.

In the spring season, with the memory of last year's dead fresh in their hearts, a band would sometimes journey to the edge of the forest, and there, in a secluded spot, they would carve the likeness of a dead relative on the bark of a smooth white poplar. Then at the foot of that tree they would leave gifts of tobacco and food and tanned skins for clothing, so that their dear one should not want for anything.

So they kept to their customs; they had the ancient stories which were handed down, besides many more that were told by mothers to their children when the shadows of evening darkened the hollow places of the prairie as if they were filled with dark water.

And I do not say that always the Kristinow did that which was good. For man is born to die, and between birth and death comes the evil Mushi-Manitou like a serpent to poison the mind.

But when there was false dealing it arose from hot blood, and not from cunning plans.

Nevertheless, no woman went husbandless, no orphan lacked shelter and food, and a murderer was banished.

There is a time to speak and a time to keep silent, and I have

1. *A Chief of the Kristinow*

2. *On the Reserve*

3. *Metal and Paper*

4. Badger

Jumping Deer

Mooswa

Redwing Blackbird

Prairie Wolf

Oriole's Nest

5. *Berry-Woman and Her Seven Sons at the Place of Tents*

6. *The Last Vision of Morning Child*

7. *Crossing Bering Strait*

told you these things, *Moosokimow*, that you may write and say: "The Kristinow did not use to live in poverty and carelessness as you see today."

I shall not speak again for many days, for there is much sorrow on me touching the last words of the story of my people, and to speak in sorrow and anger is not good.

So, for a space, till the tear be dried and the hot coal in my heart becomes ash, I shall not speak.

Morning Child signed for me to leave; and there was a nip of frost in the air, so that I shivered as I left the tepee.

CHAPTER VII

The Coming of the Strangers

When next I saw Morning Child he seemed more cheerful.
The evening was cold, and the light from the fire—a larger one
than usual—shone in turn on his face, coloring it very ruddy, and
on the grass outside, which glistened with frost. The women had
put extra robes for him to sit on, and as I entered the tepee they
were removing bowls which still savored of venison stew.

He smoked his pipe for only a short while and then launched
into his story at once.

Do not suppose (he said) that all the people of Berry-Woman
had been content to stay in the garden. Man is made full of curiosity and is drawn onward by his thoughts.

True, the Kristinow remained, for they knew in their hearts
that this was to be for them a home and a sanctuary.

But, as Berry-Woman foretold, there were those who preferred
the New Taiga, which is a land of forests and swamps, and as I
told you there were others (like the Comanches) who went south
to the dry parts. But also there were those who continued farther
east to the Five Lakes, the place of the impounding of the waters
of the flood. And in between were the O'Chippewas, and they
visited back and forth with us, and we with them.

And it came to pass that one day there came to a camp of our
people (who were beside the river) one of these. When he had
been fed and when he had finished a pipe he said: "I have been
far to the east, to the place of the Uttawah, and there I found
strange men with much hair on their faces. And see this, which
they gave me for a present?" And he brought from his belt a

mokoman, a knife. And it was not of stone, which things we had; for it was of a dark metal.

And my father's father, who was a diviner like me, a day-seer, looked and saw and said: "It is not good." And after a space the O'Chippewa departed, having nevertheless been fed and treated with much kindness.

And my grandfather was much disturbed, for, said he: "What if the people with hairy faces come to the garden with their artifacts of metal and bring confusion, as did that man of old and long ago?"

But in course of time the strangers did come, and my grandfather died and before he left us he said: "Do not forget Berry-Woman. Use the strangers well, for it is the custom. But do not touch the things of metal which they bring, for it is an offense, and these things will cause disunity."

But the manner of their coming was friendly; moreover they came from the east, from the land of *Wabun,* who brings the morning light from the realms of *peachim.* It was said that they had come from over the far water, on wings of some white stuff.

And so the Kristinow people welcomed them and sat them on bison robes, and feasted them on the humps of bison and the tail of *amisk,* the chief of the beavers.

The strangers were fair-spoken and grave in council, which was pleasing to the great chiefs and the minor chiefs and the Medicine Priests and the Old Ones and the Preferred Women—those whose husbands had been killed in war or in the chase.

And what is more they brought bright cloth and stuff such as the people had not seen before, and beads which sparkled more brightly than the quills of porcupines with which the people would trim and make gay their *popukwyans* of elk hide and their fringed leggings of buckskin.

However, as time went on, more and more of the strangers came, and they began to speak rather as masters than as friends. Then in the councils some of the Old Ones, feeling their hearts hot as coals within their breasts, fell to complaining and chiding, saying: "These pale people are killing our brothers and sisters [they meant the animals and birds], and cutting our earth friends the trees to make their forts and their fences, of which surely they have no need—if they, as they affirm, come as friends and brothers. Moreover they have no women of their own, but take to wife our maidens; then when they return to the east they abandon these women to their shame."

But others (and they were the greater number) said: "*Kaa?* What nonsense you talk! Seeing they are still few and we many. *Wha! Wha!* Perhaps the Old Ones have the hearts of women!"

So the Old Ones minded their peace, for it is not seemly for age to argue.

Time passed, and those Old Ones went to the Great Sandhills and were mourned for a space but afterward forgotten. And the new chiefs as they too became old did not remember the days before the coming of the strangers. As their eyes grew dim, they failed to notice that the score or so strangers now numbered many hundreds when joined with their allies, the men-of-mixed-blood.

As for the younger men, all but a few began to doubt the old stories and the old ways. They no longer spoke politely to the bear-people. They had forgotten Berry-Woman. And some of them threw the flesh of *amisk,* the chief of the beavers, to the dogs; and some did not take the trouble to put back the tail-tip counter of *wuchusk* into the water.

Worst of all, they began to use metal. Slowly at first; a few knives, perhaps an ax-head or two.

And since it now became clear that the People of Pale Visage had not come for friendship's sake or to find a land of peace, but rather to gather the skins of otter and beaver and lynx, and that they gave things of metal and things of cloth for these, the hunters of the Kristinow began to change their ways.

They no longer killed only for food and covering, but had to roam farther and farther afield in search of skins, betraying their earth brothers with cunning traps of metal which they obtained from the strangers.

So their eyes were dazzled and their spirit subdued by avarice and greed, and they left the good ways and forgot the ancient teachings, so that for them the garden lost its savor.

Now my father, the Stone-Gazer, came to his full stature and joined the council to sit among the Medicine Men, of which he was first. He was a night-seer, a diviner who kept in his heart all that was seemly and comely of things to do with law and marriage and little ones.

And I was then a young man and he taught me day divining; this is a light to perceive all evils of the skin and eyes, and to understand the making of camps, and of the hunt.

I had a cousin, a young girl much beloved of her uncle, my father Stone-Gazer, who had reared her because her father had died of a sickness of spots which had been unknown among us till the coming of the pale strangers.

And one of the strangers molested her, and my father was very angry, and seized the stranger (only to withhold him a little till his blood should be cooled).

But the companions of the stranger, hearing the tumult, thought it was war. They gathered with the sticks of metal which made a noise in killing, and my father was shot through the forehead, so that the blood gushed forth and he fell and departed this life.

And the strangers shut themselves within their fort and did not come out for many days.

I was not there. I learned of it when I returned from a far place where I had gone to heal a man whose skin had been torn by the claws of a panther.

But the people, in spite of my urging, would not avenge the deed. For they had become like women, and had too much fear of the smoking sticks which are called guns by the strangers, and are known by us as *paskisikun* because they shoot a bullet of metal.

So now it was found that the strangers had become too powerful, and my own people said to me: "Because of the anger of the white strangers against you, caused by their blood-guiltiness, you had better, Morning Child, remove yourself to a distance; for they call you troublemaker."

So I removed myself and stayed many years among the strange

tribes, even as far as the Dry Places. I learned a great deal and found in many places that the memory of Berry-Woman was still green.

Yet I nowhere saw a land so fair as the Garden of the Manitou where my mother bore me. So that in course of time I returned and when I had arrived within a day's march of our village I made camp in the Valley of the South Branch. That night people of the Kristinow came to me saying: "We knew of your coming, for the eagles all day have flown by two and two," which is a medicine sign.

And I said: "Do not come to me by night, for I am a day-seer and night is to me for sleep. Come rather on the morrow."

And they came on the morrow and they told me this:

"The garden which is our home has become tainted by reason of the strangers. Many things have happened. The strangers too have Men of Medicine—priests, men of valor and wisdom in many things. But they have preached that the Manitou forbids many good things, such as marrying a brother's widow. And this disturbs us, for who will hunt for such a one? Or who will give her children? This is heavy for us.

"And we have heard of great dragons which roar across the plains below the medicine line of the whites, which divides stranger from stranger and friend from friend. This dragon is a thing of metal and runs on a road of metal, and it is said that it is fed with living bison; how else should the *mustus* go yearly to the south in great herds and return in but small bands?

"And still the younger ones laugh. '*Wha!*' say they. 'We have always had the strangers, and when we do not have meat they will give us those seeds for bread and other good things. There is, moreover, a drink they have, which is better than water, for it is a living fluid. It crawls within the stomach and makes us warm. Moreover it is a laughing spirit and makes us happy. As for metal—the knives are good, and we have forgotten how to make knives of stone.'

"Thus speak the young men. And now, O Morning Child, we think the Manitou has sent you, for there is to be a council called by the strangers, and the chiefs and the Priests of Medicine are to be called together to feast with the strangers, for what purpose we know not. And we have come many miles to seek you, so that you may be present in your wisdom, to decide whether the people of the Kristinow shall best be served by way of peace or by way of war."

And I listened and pondered and said to myself: "If my people now want me, I put pride away," and with my mouth I said: "I will come." And they took me in the midst of them.

And the rest I shall tell you later.

CHAPTER VIII

The Shackling of the Kristinow

I have expected you (said the old Medicine Man a few days later). See? There is a robe! So sit while I tell a tale which is, I think, as old as the world. But because it is the end of the story of my people it is one which causes me to be sad.

Nevertheless it must be told, with all its shame. It is a story of a people who deceived, and a people who were deceived and thereby brought to nothing.

The council to which I was led, and of which I told you last time, was a very great council. It was much larger than previous councils in which we first met the few and feeble emissaries of the white strangers when *we* were the strong ones of the garden and *they* pleaded for our bounty—which was so freely given.

For at this council many were gathered. Runners had gone from camp to camp crying the news. And the chiefs and the Priests of Medicine and many of the Old Ones as well as many young warriors met together in their finest array to feast (as they thought) with the strangers.

But there were more of the strangers than was usual, and they had the red-coated soldier-police, and a bright banner, and many scribes and men of writing, and men of the Company. And there were many of mixed blood who now acted as servants to the strangers, running back and forth, arranging the seating of the council and acting as interpreters.

We had left our weapons among our tents, which is the way in council, but the white strangers (we observed) had not all done so, and the soldier-police had the short shooting sticks which hang in the belt.

But we were not afraid of them, for of all the bad things the strangers had brought to the land, they had brought two good things: the soldier-police who would never again allow an innocent man like my father to be killed without cause, and the Black-Robes who, although we could not agree with all their teaching, were gentle and kind according to their lights.

And when the evening came the white strangers left together to eat elsewhere, not dipping into the pot with us as friends do and as they had done when first they came.

And the chief of the strangers—a very great chief from the Uttawah which is by the Salt Water—showed a paper, a *mussinahi-kun,* a very strong medicine of written marks. And he said:

"O men of the Cree nation! O you chiefs and councilors! Listen!

"There is a Great Mother who wishes you well and will feed you. Behold, my hand is full of her bounty and I extend it to you! Moreover she offers a *mussinahikun* in proof. You shall grow the seeds by means of the oxen and plows we shall give you; and to this end you shall make a mark beside the marks already on the paper, and that will bring this bounty to pass. It is good, and I have spoken."

And the Old Ones and the councilors and the chiefs thought, He is speaking of our Earth Mother and her bounty, but what has she to do with making a medicine mark? And I thought, This is a trick by which I perceive that the strangers are very wise but their tongues are forked. Besides which, the one who interprets (being of mixed blood) will not explain the words well in our tongue; it is a trick to dispossess us. I have heard that the chief of the strangers is a woman, and she is the Mother they speak of.

It is in my heart that the bounty they offer is merely tawdry beads to dazzle the eyes of children and Chippewas, foolish guns to weaken the bow arms of our warriors, and bright cloth to sicken our women of tanning and fringing the buckskin which is the gift of the Manitou to us through the deer-people.

Nevertheless I shall not say too much, because my age tells me that our people have their eyes and ears stopped against wisdom. Moreover I have seen a vision of what befell the Sioux, our cousins, by resisting a *mussinahikun* below the medicine line. They provoked the wrath of the men of the *Mishi-Mokoman*— the Long Knife Soldiers. No men are more cruel than they are, since they pursue forever, cutting down both men and women with their big swords.

Therefore I will hold my peace and eat my bitter herbs alone, since to speak to no avail is not seemly.

But the Uttawah chief seemed to read my thoughts and spoke and said: "I will speak again. Listen—do you fear a trick? Do you question the bounty of the Mother? If so, will you trust your cousins and your kinfolk? Listen! The sagamores of the Uttawah have taken the bounty and say, 'It is good.' The sachems of the O'Chippewas have received the same and they say, 'It is good.' The Great Okimows of the Queen of the Rivers and of the Lake of Muddy Waters are pleased with the same and say, 'It is good.' The Uttawah father shall be your father, and the Okimowsquao— she whose servants always see the sun—shall be your Mother. It is good, and I have spoken."

Then the chiefs and the councilors withdrew with courtesy to discuss the matter of the bounty. The bounty which offered so much. Seven days they sat and took counsel one with another; the people from the Smoking Hills with the men from the Puskwa Watchee, the chiefs from Battle River with the Old Ones from the Salt Plains, those from Water-Flows-Both-Ways with kinsmen from the Eagle Mountains.

And twice each day the chief of the Mooniowuk, as the white strangers were now called, sent to ask and inquire and find out if the Cree people—the Kristinow—had yet decided. "For," the messengers said, "the hand of the Mother will not stay open forever."

But the people had reason to delay. In the first place many wished to speak and had to be permitted. It is not a small thing to speak in council and it must not be hurried. Also, many were against the bounty, for they wished to be free; but these were the older ones, for old ones' eyes are not easily dazzled. But more were for the bounty, because metal had made them contemptuous of the Old Ones and they resisted them.

Moreover, they thought, if we are not too willing, the bounty will perhaps be greater; for avarice was overcoming the spirit.

Also it was pleasant by the river and the weather was good, and there was no reason to go because there was much food and tobacco.

Each day a little—a very little—more bounty was offered; so much of this, so much of that, they were to have yearly. The Moonias-folk offered much of the *sonias* (by which they trade). First it was offered in paper, but Morning-Walker, a great chief, said: "No. Paper is the wife of metal; if a husband can string a bow, cannot a woman's tongue give the greater hurt?"

And the Young Ones said: "*Wha! Tapwā,* he is right. We shall have the white and the yellow *sonias* or none."

So they showed their confusion because of greed.

Then a blue coat was offered to each chief. The chiefs would rather have had red jackets like the soldier-police, but that was not possible, for the Mooniow chiefs knew that *red* was authority and power, and it would not do. But the chiefs were told they should have yellow braid on their coats and must be satisfied. And they would be allowed to have places for their camps, and there they would have schools and grow seeds for bread with the help of oxen and plows, which were part of the bounty.

Only—the white people would then own the prairies.

This made some of the chiefs laugh, because there was plenty of room on the prairie for their tepees, and they did not care for the seed except once in a while; and who cared who owned the prairies? They were the Manitou's. If the white people cared to say: "They are ours," that did not make it so.

And all this time I, Morning Child, appeared to doze, wrapped in my blanket and very still.

The people were told that the paper—the *mussinahikun*—gave them the right to hunt and fish as long as grass grew and water flowed. At this they laughed even more, because they did not have to be told that they could do these things, and they thought the white people very foolish to mention them.

But the strangers thought that the Cree understood what manner of changes would come, and that they laughed in glee at the promise of beads and flour and gilling twine for their nets, and for joy that they would have metal and paper, through which men obtain power.

A chief from the Moon Hills spoke and said, while the smell of sweetgrass on the fire spiced the evening air: "O my brothers and children, the *mussinahikun* promises many things and we should take the Mother's bounty. The prairies are large—we have not seen the end of them—they are wide and free. It is a small thing to let the white men call them theirs, for it cannot be. The coyote may call them his! The eagle may claim the sky! Can the white men fill them all? Can the eagles fill the air, or the fish the lake?

"Therefore I say, give them indulgence in this, for what they ask is foolish. How many of us when we were young have said to our sweethearts, 'I shall give you the moon?' Moreover, if their wrath be aroused they have other means.

"In the meantime let us take the guns and the pork and the blankets, and even the oxen and the plows, if it pleases them. The oxen we can kill and eat, while the plows will look well in front of our tepees and will be good things to tether our horses to. I have spoken."

And a chief from the Touchwood Hills spoke and said, after much talk: "There is room for all. I do not understand about the schools, but the paper promises us that our children will have the wisdom of the white men by reason of them. Also the white men's children will learn our wisdom. And we can be one people; our young men can marry their daughters and our maidens can be the wives of their men, and we can live in peace. . . ."

And the people, swaying like rain dancers, said and spoke and answered with one voice: "*Wha! Wha!* These are wise chiefs. It is good."

But a small chief from the Turtle Mountains spoke and said:

"I am going to speak. Let us hear what Morning Child says in the matter of the bounty and the medicine of marks!"

I rose slowly. And I looked about me, and I saw that the people would not be persuaded overmuch, for I said in my heart, my age tells me.

And I spoke at last, and I said: "People of the Kristinowuk, hear me! Have your elders and the great chiefs and the mighty warriors and the Preferred Women thought with care? Have they given their minds to think on your children and your children's children? Say, have they?"

And the people said: *"Uh-huh!* Yes!" and nodded, and I heard the words go like a soft wind among the people.

And I spoke again.

"I see, my children, that you have made up your minds. Had it been otherwise I might have had much to say; as it is I shall make an end of speaking."

And I sat down and drew the blanket over my face; but nobody noticed that I had not said: "It is good."

Then the council was finished. And the people of the Cree through their chiefs affixed their marks to the *mussinahikun.*

But the three chiefs of the Prairie Saulteaux with their people, the Badgers and the Gophers and the French Eaters, did not fix their marks. For the Uttawah chief had said things which did not please the cousins of the Cree; and that was because the chiefs of the Saulteaux had questioned the chief of the Uttawah overmuch. And the Saulteaux folded up their tepees and departed to the west; some to the Great House in the Rocky Mountains and some to the Sandhills of the Great Spirit Lake.

This was how the shackling of the Kristinow-people took place. This was how they came to lose the garden made for them by Weesahkahchak. This was how they became captives. This was how the mighty men and the eloquent orators and the wise councilors were confounded. They were made captive by the power of paper, which is the wife of metal.

And when the time of hunger came, the salt pork barely nourished them and even the flour of seed did not suffice. And the chiefs said, "The Manitou has covered his face by reason of metal and marks." But there were none to hear, for the young ones had cut their hair and were learning the marks.

The people of the plow, who came later in their thousands to divide the great prairie into tiny lots, did not even know the Kristinow ever had existed. The owners of the garden became as a wind that blows through grass, leaving no mark; as a fish in the water, leaving no trail; as the cry of a child in the night, after which is silence.

I have yet more to tell you, for I have had a dream and a vision, perhaps my last. But it will require much thought and prayer.

So it must wait till you come again.

CHAPTER IX

The Dream of Morning Child

Morning Child's story had interested me greatly, and it was with some impatience that I waited for word to visit him again. And then one evening I heard a soft step, and a bright-eyed boy in moccasins presented himself and said: "The oldest Medicine Man says for you to come."

So I put on a heavy coat, for it was late in the fall now. The leaves had dropped from the poplars, softly, one by one, and they rustled as I walked through them, following the wagon trail between the hills, above which the smoke of Morning Child's tepee hung white against the cold gray of the lowering sky.

The Medicine Man greeted me and accepted the tobacco I gave.

And he continued the burden of his tale, and I could see it was a heavy one, and that it relieved the stoop of his shoulders to tell it, and I gave him my attention. He spoke more slowly than usual, as if musing even as he talked.

So he began:

You have seen, Moosokimow (for that is my name among the Crees), you have seen for yourself that there are words which can be used in different ways, as a man may use a gun for a club, rather than for shooting?

So it is with a word we use—the word "good"—which you also use. And this using of words two ways can bring about confusion. Because the Cree-people thought it was good that the prairie was covered with grass; but the Moonias-people hate grass and think it is good only when the grass is buried.

And so it came about that the white strangers declared a war against the garden.

They killed the beaver-people and the marten-people and the families of otters where they played by the rivers, and the lynx and the bobcat.

And they killed the wolf-folk and the fox-folk and *mist'shaganis,* the coyote who is a voice by night. They killed all these dog-people, for they said in their rapacity and their fear, "These dog-people will eat our cattle and our stupid sheep and our scratching fowls."

But first of all they killed the bison, the humpbacked cattle of the Manitou, because they wanted the land to feed their hungry plows—those heavy things with two handles ending in a shining *mokoman,* a knife that was of steel and which bit into the earth mother's breast and turned her robe inside out.

The Old Ones in their prison yards—for they could not now go on the prairies unless they had the consent of a mark called I.D.— the Old Ones groaned against the strength of the medicine marks, all scratchy on the paper.

The Old Ones groaned and said: "It is not good. For how long, brothers and children, have *mist'shaganis* and *maheekun* the gray wolf measured the prairie with their feet, slipping between the very legs of the bison-people to find perhaps a weak calf or an ancient, dying bull? And yet did even the dog-people destroy the big-humps?

"And why should the Moonias eat little seeds like a squirrel, and grind them to make his *pakwissikun* which he calls bread, when there could be good meat enough for all, and wild onions to flavor the same, and saskatoon berries to sweeten?

"Kokiyo numooya meyasin . . . it is all bad, bad. . . ."

But the war went on.

The grasses nodded their last farewell to the father before they were buried in the cold damp earth together with the bones of the bison; both sleep, forever and together.

And, which was worse, the people-of-two-bloods, driven by hunger, gathered the bison bones before the plow to sell for a little of the metal; although by doing so they knew that their dead kinsmen would have fewer of the beasts to hunt in the Sandhills of Wapahki. And so came the saying: When meat is gone we feed on bones, like dogs.

The little folk—gophers and ground squirrels—were warred against because they ate the seeds. Soon they lay poisoned, swollen and stinking under the rays of the *kissikow peachim*. The eagle-people, the hawks and the owls fed on the carcasses and sickened and died.

And more marks were made on more papers—and the papers are the papers of the law of the white men. But this law is letters and more letters, and an Old One in a far country has said truly in the long ago that the letter killeth.

And so it was, for the letters did not know the Spirit which gives life, and so now by reason of their law the white men said, "We can kill such an animal at such a time and some we can kill at will."

And so they killed as they kill today, not for food, but because they loved to boast like children and say, "I have killed so many of such a kind."

But the animals that are not written of in this law have the more to fear, for silence is consent.

And the killing went on, and goes on. Everything that wore fur was hunted down. The badger dared not leave his den, for metal was too much for him and a steel trap was in the mouth of his burrow. The coyote dared not approach the old horse that had been shot in the bush as bait, because there might be a man with a fire-stick hidden somewhere, and a rifle barrel is a thing of metal.

The long-legged hares of the prairies—the bouncing jack rabbits —found themselves surrounded by an army of loud-voiced people who gathered the animals as a woman gathers eggs in a basket or mushrooms in an apron, until, when they were surrounded on all sides, the bloody clubs broke their skulls.

And some of the Manitou's children were called game and some vermin and some predators and some weeds, all of which can be written about on paper to make them good or bad. But it was all the same, because it did not save their lives; and of what use are names to the dead?

But there were some white men who felt with the Spirit, and these ones called all these creatures our brothers, and they also wrote on paper. But these people did not have the power of metal and there was no strong medicine in them. And some white people said, "We shall have a fund for the sky-people—the ducks and the geese and the long-legged cranes," but in truth they did not want these creatures to live except that they might kill them. Is not that a great mystery?

The forests, too, were destroyed. Axes rang day and night and steel bit deep. And this was to build house on house on house without end, clinging one to another like the nests of the cliff swallows on the cutbanks of the Great River. For man began to fear the winds of the prairie and the power of *keewadin* and he sheltered himself among many of his kind. Which is not good.

So down came the homes of the squirrel and the marten, down came the homes of *o'hoo* the great gray owl of the Strong Woods, and the *weeskipoos* and the little red crossbills. The little red crossbills who lamented and fluttered to no purpose.

And the wild cranes when they fly south each fall from the land of *keewadin,* they call and call. You will see them over the prairies, very high—circling, wheeling, reluctant to leave—calling for their friends the bison-people. But there is no answer. Only the sighing of the wind over the fields of seeds lying like burnished metal on the land.

Mist'shaganis the coyote, too, he runs and he trots and he stops and he listens. He listens for the rumbling hoofs of the bison-people and for the sound of the roaring of the bulls. And he points his nose to the *tipiskow peachim* and he sings his song of loneliness, and he stops and listens again, and there is no answer. Only the sound of the combines working at night in the harvest field. For it is metal, not blood and spirit and horns and hoofs, which is lord of the plains today.

And *mist'shaganis*? Why, *mist'shaganis* is vermin! Do not the papers of the law say so?

And so I had my vision from thinking on these things. In my vision I saw that on a later day there is to be a damming of rivers, and the waters too are to be shackled by the power of the marks and the law.

Great engines are to dig earth to stop up the great Swift Sliding river so that it cannot join its spirit to the spirits of Winnipegosis and the Salt Bay. The Moonias will say, "This is to grow more of the seed," for they say also the good rain is not enough. So the waters of the river will rise, and as they rise they will drown out the pelicans on the sandbars, and the nests of the ducks, the *sisipuk*-people, and the nests of the plovers, and the children of the kingfishers in their hollow nests.

And they will rise higher and kill the gray wolf willow and the poplar and the ash and the maple and the elm and the dogwood; all the green things which cover the banks and are a haven and a shelter to the little *apsimoosis,* the jumping deer, and the birds and the warbler-folk which make music in the glades.

And the waters will lament and say: "Did the Manitou ask us to fill the Biggest-Man-Made-Lake-in-North-America? Do not blame us, brothers, it is metal that has betrayed us all."

But the lament will be lost by reason of the boats that will dash hither and thither, faster and faster, for no other purpose than for those within to forget the Spirit, which forsakes us if we do not sit still and know the Manitou.

And the dirt from the seed fields will cover the land so as to turn red the face of *kissikow peachim* as if in anger. And the dried, sere weeds will tumble across the prairies as the moaning wind sends them hither and thither.

The red prairie lilies will try to hide from the war, but those which escape the shining blades shall be soon plucked by the hot hands of the children, only to be dropped and to lie wilted on the hard black road.

The herbs of the wayside will wither and blacken because of poison on the wind.

The children of the swallows, fed on poisoned insects, will die in the nest, and the young blackbirds in their reed cradles.

The war will go on every hour, every minute.

However, such is the power of the Spirit that a remnant and a small part will still remain of the children of the garden. And if you wish to know more about this remnant, I shall now tell you the end of my vision.

I was in the Spirit, which gives understanding, and I looked across the land. I saw the smoke from the white man's cities, and I saw the Kristinow-people in their huts of poles and mud, the hunters idle and the children not knowing their fathers.

And lo, the sky became bright, and I saw the Man of Spirit of whom the Black-Robes speak; even the Son of the Manitou. He stood upon a rainbow over and above the woman who stands with her feet on the moon. And upon His right hand and upon His left stood chiefs and sachems in their *wampum,* and men of the Black-Robes, and holy men in robes of yellow, and many more as it were a multitude. And He, the Man of Spirit, stretched out His hands. And His hands showed the marks of the nails of metal which had pierced them, even as I have seen them in the pictures of the Black-Robes. And below was a Serpent—the father of metals—and his scales were like iron and copper and the yellow metal which causes confusion; nevertheless his power was now broken by the power of a Shining One.

A great eagle, like the thunder bird, beat his wings above and around, and the eagle spoke and said: "O Morning Child, have patience yet for a time; for the strangers will tire of playing with their things of metal and will become weary, and they will yearn for the Spirit. And they will cease to torment the earth. The nails of metal, O Morning Child, have no more power. The strangers do not yet perceive this for the Serpent has deceived them. They have long known the story of the holy one and should have been children of the light, but they did not perceive the light. They did not know that the light of the Spirit is not bound, but is as a free gift to white and red alike, and that wisdom and understanding do not always wear the same robes in all places.

"Neither will the bonds of metal always have power over them and over your people, nor over our wild brothers and sisters.

"As for you, people of the Kristinow, you are people of the Spirit, and you shall increase and walk once more through fear, just as you walked through the Pass of the Hair, where I led you.

"And you shall return good for evil, and for robbery, gifts; for you shall show the strangers that evil and robbery come only through fear of fear. Fear of tomorrow, fear of the belly, fear of the body, fear of the Spirit.

"And when the strangers have walked through fear, they shall follow their Medicine Men, their Black-Robe priests, whose words they now no longer heed.

"So will the white men come to know that life is a gift—no more, no less—and a preparation for death to open the eyes forever.

"The Manitou has not covered His face as you, O Morning Child, thought in the bitterness of your heart; He has but tried your spirit and the spirit of your people. Their weeping shall cease and the people shall sing again in the time to come.

"And the white man and the red shall live as brothers, sharing wisdom whereby one does not make himself lord over others.

"The mountains shall smoke in that time as a sign, and the little hills shall skip for joy in the heat waves of *kissikow peachim.*

"And then you shall become stronger than metal; for metal must pass away when all things have been gathered and sifted by the hand of the Manitou.

"There is a time and a place, and there shall not forever be lament and sorrow and weeping for the Garden of the Manitou, the Day-Spring, the All Merciful, the God and Father of us all.

"I have said it, I that am the tongue of wisdom and the voice of the Spirit and the binder-up-of-wounds."

So spoke the eagle.

And the brightness of the skies was wiped away as a woman wipes the milk from the mouth of her babe.

This was my vision. And from it I know that to beat the air in anger will not avail. We must await the time and withstand bitterness of spirit.

And you, Moosokimow, will come again to see me when the snow falls, for I see it.

But for now, I sleep.

EPILOGUE

The snow was deep and the days were short when I visited the oldest Medicine Man for the last time.

He greeted me kindly, questioning me with his blind eyes and saying: "Have you written down the story of the Kristinow, my son?"

And I said: "I have, my father."

And Morning Child said: "It is good. Otherwise it would be forgotten. What a great thing is writing; for the words of the Old Ones are blown like autumn leaves in these days and do not enter the ears of the young men. But what you have written is written and will not pass away. It is good.

"And now, like my grandfather, I have many years, and I shall soon fall asleep.

"You are the first of the white men to listen with ears of understanding, and I think you have words behind your eyes. Always before the white men talked and would not listen, not caring to hear our words. 'For,' said they, 'these are but iseyinokans' (which is in your tongue ignorant savages) 'lacking wisdom.'

"But the wisdom of the white men is not of the spirit of the Manitou, except in small part, for the deceits of metal have blinded them as they did the eyes of the Shaman of old, the same who carried the amulet of gold.

"It is with metal that they make their trails, scorning to press with their feet the Earth Mother; with metal that they win in battle; with metal that they tell the time, not perceiving the moon and stars; with metal that they heal, knowing only the sharp needle, and scorning the comfort of the hands by which spirit speaks to spirit.

"By metal they live and by metal they die, and the wind—which is the breath of the Kisā-Manitou—passes unheeded over and about their high tepees of wood and stone and metal.

"You are the first to have listened, and your words will not be understood until a time has gone by; until the heart of man cries to be bound up as a wound that bleeds, and a gaping wound. And that will not be until the white man has tired of playing with his toys of metal and has suffered many things by reason of them, so that he will yearn again for the spirit of the father and the mother. Even as was said to me in the vision."

As Morning Child spoke I looked again at the last mark on his robe. It was a mark of metal, and yet not completely that, for it was more like an idol and it included something of smoke too— much smoke and darkness.

On his robe was no space left, and even as I looked I knew that the snow would now cover the last footprint of Morning Child forever, and that his mouth would speak no more.

And now (for he had closed his eyes) he sighed a little, and smiled a little, then opened his eyes toward me to look kindly (though indeed he was blind). And his spirit departed to the Sandhills of Wapahki. And I was glad that Morning Child would now stand with the tall chiefs in their *wampum* and feathers who bow down before the Master of Life.

So I left the camp and went back to my own people. And there a man accosted me and said: "I hear that the old troublemaker, the Indian witch doctor, is dead. Just as well. Always stirring things up with his stories about the good old days, before the Reserves. It'll be better when all his sort are gone. Then perhaps we can civilize the Indians."

I knew he meant my friend Morning Child. But I said nothing; for I remembered that the man who spoke had a great deal of schooling, and that because of his studies he had put away compassion and understanding for the dry crusts of facts and figures and graphs.

And I remembered further that spirit cannot talk to facts, and that the oldest Medicine Man had said: "To argue is not seemly."

IN THE SIGN OF THE BEAR

Only by Faith we find the golden gleam
. . . the candles of the dawn.
To light the temple of the soul's desire.

CHARLOTTE CLEMENTS

Green Arrows

PREFACE

This is a story. Neither more nor less.

You may, if you wish, call it a fairy tale, especially if you can feel fairies in rushing waters, in wind-blown grass, in falling snowflakes, and in the mists of the tundra. Like all fairy tales, it tells of high endeavor rewarded by happy achievement.

What is true, what is timeless, what is world-wide, is the dual foundation on which the tale is built.

In these days of conveniences and aids, we are apt to forget that man is born with just such instincts as make survival possible for animals and that the loss of these instincts has come about as the result of what we call civilization. In civilization a child's every want is at once fulfilled, so that these instincts (occasionally appearing as "hunches") not being called upon, or discouraged by the proponents of security, quite naturally become atrophied.

There is nothing remarkable about an animal finding its way without maps and compasses. There is nothing remarkable about an animal's ability to distinguish between wholesome and harmful berries or roots; it is enough to test the flavor or texture. As to shelter, an animal can at once recognize the cave, the hollow log, or the lee of a snowdrift as a haven in times of wind or storm.

So, once, could our remote forefathers see the fulfillment of their basic needs in their immediate surroundings.

But man, by his intellect, has so perfected his way of life that he has less and less use for the art of knowing direction by the eye, by a "feeling" for the lie of the land, for the great clock in the sky or the wind that he muffles himself against.

Unlike animals, men like to think, to weigh, to conclude, to plan, to prepare.

It is our nature and right. Yet sadly, we go so far in pruning and watering and training our powers of reason that by reason we say an action or a plan is impossible at worst or fraught with too much danger at best. For we have lost the old survival instinct, something very closely akin to faith in ourselves and our environment.

The wandering nomad walks without fear, even though aware of his mortality and alert to danger.

He walks without fear as the caribou herd or the zebra troop walks without fear; for if they were possessed by fear, life would be hell indeed. When fear does come at last it is too late to matter. The skin boat has overturned, the trigger has been pulled, the lion has charged; after which is darkness.

On these two, the instinct for direction and the instinct for recognizing edibles and shelter, depends the survival of animals and untutored man. These are the gifts bestowed on man and beast alike at their very conception.

The story has no moral, except perhaps to suggest that the world and all therein is good and comely and was never meant to be a place of torment and pain or of futile and unrewarded struggle.

CHAPTER ONE

1

The little plane sideslipped, stuttered, recovered, and droned on. The third time in ten minutes, thought Elspeth, and looked down once more as she had done so many times since they had left Edmonton. But all below was shrouded by the snow which was falling in feather-size flakes.

She knew what should lie beneath the thick clouds. This was not her first trip to Coronation Gulf. By her reckoning they should be well beyond the belt of scattered timber which bordered Great Slave Lake, and below—if she could only see—should lie the dull white of the late winter barrens.

She glanced briefly at the pilot's head, less than two feet ahead of her. His shoulders looked determined and confident enough, and she checked the impulse to bother him with questions which would have to be shrieked above the noise of the engine and the wind in the struts.

Instead, she looked down again at her child, wrapping the white woolly blanket more firmly about the little thing sleeping so confidently in her arms, his tiny breath rising like a thin mist from the small gap she had left in the soft material.

How pleased his policeman father would be.

"It's got to be a boy, mind you," he had smiled as he helped her into the plane which had taken her "outside."

She had wanted the baby to be born at Coronation, a true "son of the North," but Bruce had vetoed that.

"Edmonton for you," he had said. And what he said was law to Elspeth. He knew the Arctic.

That had been five months ago and she was impatient to see him again and to show him his son.

2

The roar of the engine ceased . . . then started again, but unevenly. In that brief moment of utter silence Elspeth felt a sudden premonition of disaster.

The light was failing now.

In spite of her resolution (You must have faith, she thought) she reached forward and touched that close, broad shoulder.

The engine stopped again, spluttered, and died.

The pilot turned his head. She could faintly see one blue eye peering at her around the edge of his frost-rimmed ear flaps.

"Off course," he said. "Sorry. Out of gas, I'm afraid. I'm going to make a landing. Hold tight, eh?"

Elspeth could not tell if they were going up or down, but felt the machine shudder and heard the wind scream. Her last connected thought was more of a prayer—Oh, God, take care . . .

That was all.

And somewhere in the Canadian wilderness between the Coppermine and Bathurst Inlet a small plane lay like a broken dragonfly among a jumble of lichened outcroppings while slowly, flake by moon-white flake, the snow obliterated the last traces, and the shattered parts became one more well-kept secret of the featureless landscape.

3

The old couple huddled low in the lee of the great rock. Here was a little patch of harsh, frozen ground which the falling snow could not reach. They had not been able to keep up with the band of Innuits which had passed here, was it yesterday or many days ago? They did not know.

They had been left a little oil, some dried meat, and a tattered caribou robe. The food was gone now and they awaited the end, huddling close, more from companionship than for the benefit of the feeble warmth they might share, for death is a lonely thing even when pain leaves, as it does at the last.

The sound of the falling plane seemed no more to their dull ears than the wingbeats of a white owl. But the crash of metal on rock alerted the two, or one at least. For when the old man stood up he knew that his wife, still half squatting, could not rise with him.

He stooped painfully and laid her down, knees bent, on her side.

Leaving the dead woman, he moved feebly toward the blur of black which lay, grotesquely bent, among the snowy rock humps.

He was not frightened. He recognized what he saw as one of the flying *komatiks* of the white man; and now he searched for what he might find. A dead man. He grunted. A dead woman, a white woman, and he grunted again. She was young and evidently healthy, for she was fat too.

Then he saw that she was not so fat, after all, but that she had her arms locked tightly about something. On his knees now, he felt and pulled.

Then it was in his arms and he felt a sense of disappointment, for it was not a bundle of food, for how could dried meat wriggle and cry out? And he knew.

He was about to drop it in the snow, for, with the mother dead, the child too must perish. That was the way of the hungry barrens; but just then he tripped on something. It was a duffel bag of sorts. He thrust in his arms and felt cans; one, two cans. That, he knew, was white man's food. And not frozen yet, for the bitter cold of deep winter had passed, and the sun now showed above the horizon a little more day by day.

Slowly, laboriously, carrying the baby and the cans, he made his way back to where his dead woman lay, noticing in a dull way that the small patch of overhung ground where they had sheltered narrowed at the back between the rocks, as if it led to some place.

Perhaps a bear den. An old one, for his dim eyes could pick

out no tracks, and at this season a bear should be bestirring itself, at least to sun itself a little each day—unless it was a she with cubs.

The child cried again, and with its cry the old man thought again of food, as he had not thought of it for many days.

What kind of food, he wondered, would be in the cans? And how does the white man get it out? He bashed a can on the rock with his waning strength, but the metal only dented.

He tried dropping a stone on it with no better result. If he had a knife now; and with that thought he felt about for and found a sharp piece of broken stone. Using another larger rock, he pounded the sliver two or three times into the top of the can and was rewarded by a slow trickle of something thickly liquid.

Carefully he tasted it. Sweet, oh, so sweet it was, like the caribou milk he had tasted after he had killed a nursing doe. He put the can to his lips and drank a little and then, smearing a finger with the stuff, he pushed it dripping between the baby's lips.

The crying ceased and the little lips sucked ecstatically. Again and again the starving old man, knowing that he was at the end of the long journey of life, fed the small man whose foot had not yet taken the first step.

Through the blackness of that night, while the soft snow fell all around, the ancient and the infant slept together, the one too old to care for the morrow, the other too young.

4

It was nearly noon of the next day when they awoke. The snow had stopped, the clouds were breaking, and it was cold with the damp chill of late March.

The child was crying again and the old man opened the other can very slowly, for his strength was dwindling, overtaxed as it had been from last night's exertions. But this can was a different shape and had flowery colors on it. After all his exertions, it yielded only some pink dust which gave off a smell like a summer's day. It was so dry to his gums that he could not stomach it, and as for the child, it cried harder than ever when he tried to force some between the blue little lips.

The old man squatted, staring into the pallid distance, slightly rocking the little thing across his knees.

And as he peered with his sightless eyes, something made his nostrils twitch. It was a smell, and smells are rare in the cold barrens. The reek of an animal, acrid, musky, and warm with life.

It came from behind him. From deep within the narrow fissure that he had first noticed the previous evening.

Slowly, on one hand and his knees, the child held close to his sunken chest, he squeezed between the rocks and found himself partly within a den, and he knew it was occupied, for the reek was stronger and the air held a steamy warmth.

He did not care, did not even consider whether the occupant was a he- or a she-bear. It would be a warm place for the little one when he was gone. Not such a lonesome place for a child to die as out there. . . .

He placed the bundle, blanket and all, beside a great shaggy flank of coarse yellowish-white hair and retreated backward as slowly as he had entered.

By the time he had curled up beside the body of his wife, facing her back, his knees bent like hers, the low sun was stretching pink fingers across the tundra. The rays played briefly upon the old man's face, etching deeply the crisscross of wrinkles and the shadowed eye-sockets.

The old man's lean cheeks and wrinkled forehead were suffused for a moment. He put his arm across the old woman's shoulder and pressed her close. *Ayolarama,* he thought sleepily. It is the end.

So they lay together, as they had lain so many nights since the day when he, a young and active hunter, had first taken her, a comely maiden, to his winter igloo.

CHAPTER TWO

1

Nook was a mighty hunter, and Nook had boasted to the Company clerk that he would bring a fine white bearskin to the post if he could get a supply of ammunition and other necessities on "jawbone," for his fall hunt might be a long one.

The clerk demurred. There had been too much credit given out the fall before. It was high time more furs came in. Nook explained smiling that he had not been among that bunch of shorewise fish eaters who had used their jaws and tongues so glibly when it came to making promises.

Well, the clerk wanted a polar bear rug for his mother in Winnipeg, and although it was against the rules, he advanced the goods on his own credit.

2

Now Nook, several weeks later, was far to the east, traveling light with his few necessities packed on the backs of his loose running dogs. Traveling was easy, for the summer had been warm, melting all the snow except for a few drifts in the hollows.

On the caribou hunt of the previous fall, after the first light snow, he had seen a bear track and, with winter imminent, a she-bear (he knew it by her sign) would be fattened on the tundra berries and would soon den. At that season her coat should have been prime. Nevertheless he had abandoned the track and gone back to caribou hunting with his people; for that was custom. But he remembered; and this fall he would not join the tribal caribou hunt. He had asked, and his brother-in-law would hunt for him; for he, intent on bigger game, had left the tents well before the first early snows.

He camped tonight by a small rivulet, now dry. It drained a height of land he remembered. A few tiny willows, scarcely knee-high, gave some shelter from the cool fall wind which already held a hint of winter; and the few dry twigs which he had laboriously gathered now hissed and spat in a small fire.

He knew he was close to where he had seen the track almost a year before. She-bears, he knew, denned late if they had borne cubs during the winter darkness, and since this one had had no cubs last year (for he had found no cub tracks), she should certainly have a cub or cubs this season. For two years past the berries had not been in their former abundance, nor had marmots been plentiful, and by these signs Nook expected only one cub, if she had any. In time of great plenty, he remembered, they often had three, although two was the common number. This she, then, should not be far away. A male bear now, that was different. They stirred early and late. One might be here in the fall and far out on the polar ice by summer.

Turning these things over in his mind, Nook called his dogs about him and composed himself to the half-sleeping, half-waking rest of a hunter.

3

Nook was recalled to full wakefulness by the croak of a raven, and his heart rose. Ravens seldom stray far from some hunting animal; for it is largely upon their leavings, or the mice they disturb, that the black birds sustain life.

Something was near, that was certain. Perhaps only a fox or a lean wolf—or perhaps a bear, digging for a fat marmot or feeding on some carrion.

As he thought of this, the raven croaked again and was joined by another. They circled above him for a minute or two, the one occasionally rolling with a flip of his sable wings, uttering an almost musical note, while the other, unimpressed and not deceived by the springlike morning, began to draw away toward the stone-jumbled height of land more than a mile away. Soon the two became mere specks, flying slowly, one just behind the other.

Without haste, for haste is the hunter's betrayer, Nook munched his dry meat, while his dogs looked on hungrily, their wet snouts following the movement of his hands, their jowls drooling.

But dogs must be fed only at the end of their day's work, for after a morning feed they become as sleepy and sluggish as a full-bellied wolf.

Slowly, carefully, Nook lashed his packs to the dogs' backs, counting every item. A little flour, some salt, two sacks of dried meat, tea, sugar. His tinderbox and ammunition were kept in the fold of his parka lining.

Carefully he withdrew his rifle from its caribou-skin scabbard and inspected it closely.

Satisfied, he slung the rifle over his shoulder, tucking the soft scabbard into his belt.

Then he spoke to the burdened dogs and stepped out in long easy strides toward the ridge, now outlined in dark blue against the saffron sky.

4

Nook had put barely half a mile between himself and his late camp when one of the dogs dashed forward, stopped with his nose to the ground, and began to scratch. It was soon joined by the others, all tumbling about in a flurry of waving tails. Reaching the spot, Nook found himself staring at bear sign, dark with the pulp of autumn berries. Though now affixed by the night frost to the hard, dry ground, he knew it was recent.

The ravens had not lied, he thought.

Taller than his dogs, Nook could look over the small hillock at the foot of which they had stopped. He could quite clearly see the jumble of gray-black rock which was the shoulder of the ridge before him.

Examining its length from left to right, he could see a pale patch which he first took for a belated snowbank, but as he looked it moved slowly to the right, and he made it out to be a bear. At that distance he could not tell whether it was alone or not.

There is my white bear robe, he thought, and looked for a way to approach closer.

Just to his right a little watercourse, now dry, zigzagged toward him down the slight rise of ground, all fringed with ripe cotton grass. Probably, he conjectured, it joined the little creek by his camp.

He called his dogs and strode toward the shallow gully, noting with satisfaction that its sides became higher as he progressed upward.

Soon he was almost at its source among the black boulders between which tussocks of coarse grass nodded dryly in the morning breeze.

Quietly he clambered up the bank and peered over the top.

There was his bear thirty yards away, rooting among the stones, turning over the smaller ones for beetles, grubbing out tubers or lemming broods. He unslung his rifle and waited.

The beast's back was toward him and he had no wish to spoil that silky hide; he must wait for a heart shot.

Then he saw the cubs. Two. Gamboling among the brittle scarlet stems of stunted fireweed.

The bear turned sideways, her nose toward the little playmates; and at that moment Nook pressed the trigger.

His dogs, panting, broke into a chorus of staccato barks, and as he rose and approached the bear, rifle ready, they bounded forward as fast as their packs would allow and surrounded the evidently dying animal.

Chary of wasting ammunition, and not wishing to spoil the hide of his prize unnecessarily, Nook merely covered it with his sights; but no second shot was needed.

The dogs, after a cursory sniff at the blood, now turned their attention to the cubs, one of which stood up, bear fashion, and whimpered.

Nook raised his rifle and the cub fell. The young meat would be good, and these two would soon perish without their mother.

The circle of dogs now drew back a little, puzzled, looking from the second cub back to Nook; for it was no cub and gave out the man smell.

Nook rubbed his eyes. What was that little creature on all fours, dragging a piece of something that looked like ragged cloth?

He approached slowly, while his dogs, growling deep in their throats, pressed close behind him. Then Nook laughed, as such men do when puzzled and embarrassed, for he recognized the little creature as a human child, perhaps a year old, but like no such little person as he knew back in his village. For its hair was red, not black, and it would have been naked but for the strip of torn and soiled blanket it clutched.

He swept the child into his arms, hardly feeling the quick bite which his hand received from the hard little gums set with a few tiny milk teeth.

Taking a length of sealskin line, Nook quickly trussed the little boy (for the child was a male) and, oblivious to its whimpering sobs, started skinning the she-bear. He noticed that her dugs still held milk, but little, and surmised that the cubs had been for some time now less dependent on those fountains than on seeds, berries, and roots, and perhaps even meat.

Having finished his task, he placed the bear's bloody skull high on the rocks, for she was, after all, an ancestor and entitled to this attention.

Then he skinned out the cub, taking the hindquarters for a stew, before he retraced his steps toward the camp, the flapping hide a greater burden for his shoulders than the child was for his arms. The cub skin, wrapped around the pink meat, he packed on the largest and strongest dog.

At his camp among the willows he unpacked the beasts and turned them loose. They would return to the bear carcass and eat their fill. He would not need them the next day anyway, for he would have to trim and flesh the hide and fold it into a more comfortable shoulder pack.

While a stew simmered in his black kettle he untied the child, speaking softly and avoiding with a laugh the little hands which clawed at him and the mouth that tried to bite. Holding it firmly, he took his whalebone spoon, filled it with gravy, blew a few times to cool it, and pushed it between the close-clenched jaws of the infant. At first he tried to spit it out, but finally, won by the delicious taste and the familiar bear smell, he began to swallow the gruel greedily.

5

The Innuit camp was a small one of only a dozen summer tents. These formed a little circle on a tussock-strewn piece of flat land separating the beach from the black boulders rimming the tundra which rolled south but little above the level of the salt water of the narrow inlet.

Snow had fallen before Nook's return, and the brown and scarlet of the tiny shrubs and dry low-growing arctic flowers only just overtopped the white stuff sufficiently to give the landscape a speckled appearance. Where the wind had blown off some slope these, and the dun grasses, looked like scattered bits of carpet; and where the same hand had left the rock faces bare, driving the snow into the fissures, the low escarpment resembled an abstract design in black and white.

The little tents of caribou hide, held up by crookedly forked sticks, together with the tramped and sullied snow between, made a smudgy stain on the white scene, while the smoke of cooking fires rose darkly into the bright, clean air above.

The pack ice beyond the inlet was freezing together, and it would not be long before the dark salt water became itself a frozen plain, a hunting ground from which seal and walrus could be garnered.

6

The autumn caribou hunt had been a good one, and the drying
racks were full of meat. Even now some was already sufficiently
dry to be pounded to shreds between smooth stones, and many
women were thus engaged preparing a supply for winter use.

And Nook was back. He and his hunt, but especially the finding
of the child, were the talk of the camp. The Old Ones said it was
not good that a white child—and raised by a bear at that—should
be with the Innuit, the People.

There had been an Indian child once, an old crone remembered.
An Indian child—she spat—a young savage; *he* had been found
on a hunt that went too far to the south, to where the trees stood
on end like posts instead of lying peaceably on shore. There,
some of the strange people, the enemy, had been camped and the
child had been abandoned. The Innuit had cared for it, and what
had *it* done? Brought a bad sickness to them from which many,
and the small bearer himself, had died in great pain. . . .

But that was long ago.

And the Young Ones, what should they know of long ago?
Each generation must learn its own lessons. That was what the
Shaman said, and after he had looked at the entrails of an un-
mated caribou cow, he had said: "Let him be tested, for I see no
wrong here."

First the Shaman looked long and hard at the dirty rag which
the child refused to be parted from, and, taking one end, turned
it this way and that until he came to the marks woven with faded
blue thread in one corner, thus: $\lambda \wedge$.

This he drew thrice in the snow with a finger, while the people
strained forward to see. Meanwhile the child had clung firmly to
one end of the rag, crying, but as the Shaman dropped the end
he had seized, the child subsided and sat hugging the thing to
him. Then the Shaman plucked three hairs from the child's head,
plaited them together with a few bents of dry grass from his

wizard's bag, spat on them, and tossed them into the still air. Whirling like a shuttlecock, the little bundle hurtled down and landed on the piece of cloth now spread in front of the child, whereat he crowed with delight and began to play with the bundle, tossing it high.

Still not completely satisfied, the Shaman walked three times around the little group of onlookers, one hand over his mouth, shaking a rattle and groaning. Then with a sudden yell he stopped, fumbled in the bag hung around his neck, and threw the magic walrus tooth directly at the child's head. It grazed his cheek and fell with a thud behind his right shoulder, the shoulder which activates the arrow-hand.

The Shaman picked it up and studied it carefully for a moment. It had landed with the rune side up, the side all carved with strange marks that only a Shaman can interpret.

Slowly he turned to the people, his face a mask, his eyes closed. After a moment's silence he spoke: "Let the child stay with the Innuit. The bear is an ancestor, and there is a purpose. Till *he* chooses, he stays.

"The magic grass says so. See, he clutches it and is not afraid! The magic walrus tooth given to our ancestors by She-Down-There says so. The rag of strange wool—for it is not musk-ox wool—says so, for do ye not see for yourselves," he pointed to the marks in the snow, "do ye not see that he walks in confidence to our tents, and later perhaps to other tents, in peace?" And he began a chant which was old when the Innuit were young:

> "I will take care not to go towards the dark,
>   for I will go always toward the light."

7

So the child stayed. And it ceased to growl or to bite, and grew fat on marrow and broth, and learned to speak as people speak and stood upright; and soon any memory of the cave and the shaggy nursemaid passed away so that he thought he had been born in the camp, and that Nook and his plump wife were his parents (for indeed they had been childless and made much of him).

Only sometimes, if the sleeve of his jacket was rucked up, one of the little camp boys would put a finger on the white scars which crisscrossed each other on the pale skin of his forearms. And secretly he would sometimes take off his sealskin boots and touch the same kind of scars on his shins, and frown and try to remember. But he could not.

Once also, when a hunter had killed a bear with young cubs out on the ice—for the beasts sometimes denned in such places—and came to camp and threw down the small bleeding body he had taken from her, he had stood looking till his chest ached and his nose felt hot and then suddenly had burst into tears, a thing no proper Innuit child would do.

But he did not know why he had done so, and was ashamed and hid himself.

CHAPTER THREE

1

It was in this manner that the strange infant became part of the band of caribou Innuit who lived mostly inland, only visiting the coast on occasion. These hunting grounds were rarely visited by strangers of any kind and the knowledge of white men and their ways had come to them late.

In what little contact they had with the post at Coronation, the child was not mentioned, for it would be better, the Shaman had told them, to keep it to themselves. He reminded them that —as many older ones would remember—the white man was unpredictable. Only fifteen years before, two of their number had killed a white shaman, a priest, near the Copper River, from fear only, for he was the first white they had seen and they had misinterpreted his purpose.

Soon after, a tall man with yellow striped pants, together with three more warriors like himself, had come and talked much and said they must not interfere with whites at any time; for the whites were powerful and under the protection of a great banner, such as flew at Coronation, and they (the yellow-stripes) were the servants of the banner, and had authority over life and death.

And they said that under the banner all killing of men was forbidden and could be punished by hanging. Indeed, they had said that it was in their hearts to hang the two, but because the two had not known these things, they would spare them, taking pity on their ignorance.

And, went on the Shaman, it was a hard thing for the Innuit, seeing that, if the banner forbade all killing, how could its servants kill by hanging?

All this time two of the older men sat very still, for they were embarrassed, and they put their hands over their mouths.

Moreover, the Shaman had concluded, there had now been, for several years, a yellow-leg man at Coronation, and it would be best he did not know of the child, for fear that there be an accusation of theft, which the banner might think even worse than killing. And who among the whites (being but new-come, and knowing the ways of neither Innuits nor bears) would believe how the child had come to them?

Silence would be better.

2

They called him by a long name all made into one word, a name which means: "He came by way of a Bear Ancestor"; this strange white-skinned boy who could cry as their children could not. They only complained when they were hurt or hungry; not like this one, who became disturbed for nothing! But mostly they shortened the name to Nanuk, which means "A Bear."

The boy talked quite well at three; he could run and jump and play with the best, yet after play was over he often sat by himself, silent, looking; always looking toward the day. Always so eager and happy when the village moved south into the tundra to hunt the caribou.

Sometimes on these hunts they went as far as the stick country, from which they brought back many things not found on the coast. But not if Indian sign was around. The Indians were—different. They were . . . savages . . . they attacked without warning and for no reason. There were deer enough for all.

And moreover, these Indians called them, the Innuit, by a name which means "cannibal," although the eating of human flesh was an abhorrent thing to the People—except when a Shaman had need to commune with the world of spirits. That was a different matter and not to be questioned.

3

Nanuk (to shorten his name) was squatting in the snow outside a winter igloo when the white man came. He was three years old now, and he was playing with a few strands of musk-ox tail hair, making a little harp by tying them across a forked willow twig.

The village saw the stranger while he was still far off. The low winter sun, just peeping over the horizon as the hour of noon approached, threw his long shadow and that of his dogs almost to the camp.

They knew him for a white man. An Innuit would have traveled in company with others, and his dogs would not be drawing an Alaskan sled with its high sides and pole brake.

The stranger halted his dogs some distance from the camp and approached with long strides. In halting Innuit he told them he was from the coast. This they had already guessed, although he came from the south. And they also knew that he was the yellow-leg man from Coronation.

He asked many questions. He wanted to know if they had found the carcass of a flying *komatik* during their travels in the barrens. One had been lost, he said; had been lost for three years. He who asked the questions had never ceased trying to find it. He had visited all the bands of people for many miles and they, at this village, were the last. He had supposed they hunted too far to the southeast, but still they might have seen or heard something. But no, the people said, they had found no such thing. If they did, they would send word to Coronation if that were possible, but sometimes they were far away for as long as two years.

Then the policeman asked if he could get a little meat for his dogs, and camp overnight with them, and they said yes. He would be welcome.

He stayed with them that night, and was preparing to leave next morning, harnessing his dogs by moonlight although it was already late. Nook and some others were standing about watching him and talking and laughing among themselves, and as the policeman turned to bid them good-by, a small boy came from behind the group and approached him shyly, staring. It was not until the little fellow had grasped him boldly by the stripe on his breeches that the white man noticed him.

Looking down, he gazed full in the child's face.

He looks very white, he thought, and made to push back the boy's parka hood. He just got a glimpse of what might have been blue eyes when the youngster backed away. The policeman's lips began to frame a question, but just then he noticed Nook looking at his woman, who was coming toward the boy. It was a long, peculiar look and their eyes met, the man's and his woman's. Misinterpreting the crafty, sideways glance, the white man killed the words on his lips. Moonlight plays strange tricks; and so do white men sometimes. Especially in native camps. Instead of speaking he began to fill his pipe, then passed the pouch to Nook, who put a wad in his mouth and passed it to the next.

Soon all were murmuring and chewing happily, while the policeman thought of how often he had seen near-white children among the bands; the result of an indiscretion or perhaps wife-lending.

He was pleased he had not inquired further, for he had no wish to offend.

Now he picked up his long whip, spoke to his dogs and, stepping on the back of the sleigh, cracked the whiplash and was gone. But as he looked over his fanned-out dogs, each with its tail curled over its quarters, as he listened to the whine of his sledge runners, and as the thickly gathered stars began to pale and the sky to the south began to brighten, he felt uneasy.

He felt that something was undone, something waited, something tried to speak to him, and his thoughts were drawn willy-nilly toward the woman he would never see again.

"Time for a transfer," he said aloud, and his lead dog answered with a low whine and increased the pace.

CHAPTER FOUR

1

Nanuk was fifteen the year they had to go farther inland than usual to find the deer herd; and in a different direction too, more easterly; because, for some reason best known to the big-antlered herd leaders, the animals had swerved from their usual migration route. So a great deal of time was lost before the first beds and feeding grounds were found.

Nanuk was already taller than many of the rather squat villagers and was still growing rapidly. But he was much slenderer of bone—"wrists like a woman," someone said. His height was more in his legs, too, and that was something to smile at; for "long-legs" was the theme of a certain old story, to be told on winter nights, and when the women were sleeping.

But the lad was no fool, the Old Ones agreed. He had a way with dogs that no show-off young Innuit, for all his sharp tongue and skill with the long, braided dog whip, could match.

Then again, in the matter of fire, no one of his age could handle the stick and bow so well. He was an apt pupil, the Shaman found, and he understood many things which puzzled other boys of his age, even those who could outdo him in the arts of the chase.

He was much more content to listen to the Old Ones; quick to sense their moods and wishes, and asked many questions. And he went off much by himself. "Let him," said the Shaman. "He has much to find behind his eyes. Already his ancestor spirit tells him that he is not a true Innuit. See how he walks! We do not swing our arms that way."

2

The Innuit hunted late that fall, penetrating farther toward the stick country than usual. Several snowstorms had come and gone, but with the unusually mild weather the ground was now bare, although it was well into November.

Late one afternoon Nanuk became separated from the other hunters as he followed a fine caribou bull, one he had wounded with an arrow. It had not died at once, but plunged away to the south, toward a patch of trees standing thicker than usual. It disappeared and he followed it for over a mile. He did not press it close, for he knew that before long it would lie down. Then its wound would stiffen and he would get another shot.

He left the open, or semi-open, country in which they had found the herd and found that the thicket was in low ground where the trees were a little taller. He threaded through the close growth of young spruce and came into the open again. He could not see the deer but heard a raven croak still farther south and knew his game was there. When he did come upon it, it was dead, lying sprawled in another hollow where stunted willows grew.

Now he knelt to skin his prize and as he slit the animal's hide from throat to tail he could still hear, but faintly, the shouts of the hunters behind him.

Carefully he skinned out one side and turned the carcass on to it, keeping everything clean as he started on the other. He had a good knife. Not a stone one but a good steel knife Nook had got for him from the Company.

As he slit the skin upward from the big hind tendon, he felt a flake of snow on the back of his neck, another on his bare hand. He looked up. The sky was dark, speckled with the white spots which now came thicker and faster. He could no longer hear the voices of his friends.

Then came a gust of wind, followed by another, and he felt

suddenly cold where before the still air had been quite warm on his cheeks.

The raven which had been watching him from a distance was nowhere in sight.

Darkness was coming on, and with it came a still fiercer wind which tore at the small willows and shrieked in the few scrubby spruces which stood near by.

By the time he had finished his job it was dark, the fluffy flakes had become as small and sharp as sand, and he could see no farther than the length of a whiplash in any direction.

Nanuk felt no fear; hardly annoyance. No Innuit is impatient, for weather is beyond changing. He would have to wait out the storm, that was all. He had a small tea pail at his belt, he had his knife and his bow. He had meat here in plenty and a caribou skin which, propped on the lee side by a few sticks, would freeze and hold its shape as a windbreak; and the Labrador shrub grew in abundance here, so he would not want for a hot drink.

He had no fire drill, but that could soon be remedied, for with his knife he could soon make one with a piece of straight spruce for the upright, his bow for power and a piece of the half-rotten wood which lay underfoot for tinder.

It took him some time to make his simple instrument, working in almost total darkness, but his fingers were sensitive and he felt his way.

Having got his soft piece of punk wood, he rotated his stick under the shelter of the hide which he threw over some willows. Under this shelter, his spark—when it came—would not be dampened by the falling snow. He had already placed in readiness a handful of dry moss and a double handful of small twigs broken from the spruce trees.

He was rewarded for his labors by a little puff of smoke, then a glowing of the punk wood.

Hastily he placed some scraps of moss on the piece, crumbling it with his fingers, blew three or four times till they burst into flame, and began to add a few twigs, building them up in a small cone. Soon a little fire no bigger than his hand crackled. All he had to do now was to keep it fed, and he gathered deadfall and dry limbs for an hour, questing farther and farther afield as the light of his fire flared.

As he finished his strip of broiled venison, his tea pail boiled over and he removed it, setting it down to cool a little, and letting the pungent and aromatic steam from the leaves of the Labrador shrub curl up around his face.

Suddenly he started. Something brushed his shoulder and a cold nose was thrust against his.

It was Ahneek, his favorite among Nook's sleigh dogs; the big yellow one with the dark patches around his eyes and on his flanks.

The big dog looked north into the blizzard and whined. "No," said the boy, "we camp here tonight," and threw his companion a rib bone.

CHAPTER FIVE

1

The storm lasted all the next day and into the night, during which Nanuk made shift to keep his fire going. On the second morning he woke to the whining of Ahneek. The boy rose and, cutting off a fat caribou rib, pierced it with a sharp stick by which he held it over the hot coal till well broiled.

While he ate, and later as he began to pack his few belongings, the dog walked back and forth, scratching at the snow, looking always to the north, and turning to push Nanuk with his nose, making little yelps.

Nanuk disregarded the animal's urgency. During the night he tried to think out something which had long disturbed him.

He felt unhappy. Nook and his wife, the Shaman, and all the people had been good to him. Very good, he remembered.

Yet always there was an urge within him which said he must leave them, but for what, even now he did not know. To find another people? Where? Not north surely, for few lived there; east and west he knew, but that too was Innuit land.

South? He knew nothing about the south. It was the land of the highest light. The light that always seemed to beckon him, toward which his spirit strained. Why?

And why did he yearn for another people? What people?

What did it mean?

Had it to do with his coloring? His features? So different from the other people.

Bears, foxes, caribou, he thought, had young exactly like themselves. The other children of the camp resembled their parents. But he was not like Nook, nor the wife of Nook and the whites—

the Big Eyebrows (as they were called)—were said to have blue eyes, not dark eyes with their sparse eyebrows like the Innuit.

He knew in his heart, from hints, from looks, from the teasing of other children, that his beginning was not as theirs. His name even . . . but he was not really at all like a bear, surely. Yet the name meant something like the Sign of the Bear . . . the Ancestor.

He was sadly puzzled by the conflict within. But always that inner voice said: Now is your chance to find out. Already you are well on your way. Press on, follow the light, let the day be your guide and your goal; go toward it.

What could be there? Was it some part of him from which he had become separated? Was the land to the south like this; just small scrub, sickly little trees, a gray horizon lost in fog? Or was it . . . different? Would there be big trees like those lying on the northern beaches, brought, it was said, by the Great River to the west? Surely there must be people. There were savages, he knew, but it could not be they who drew him on, surely? No. He would have to avoid them if he went.

If he went?

The thought of turning north again gave him no feeling of pleasure, although he loved Nook and Nook's wife. For years he had thought of her as his mother, but now he could not. That the Innuit would look for him he did not doubt; that they would find him he doubted. The storm had destroyed his tracks, and he had been warned not to go too far into the scraggly timber. They would hardly look for him there. And if they did, he told himself with a sudden flash of resolution, they would not find him.

2

His mind made up, Nanuk tucked his knife carefully under his skin parka, wrapping it in the folds of the rag which he always wore next to his body like a sort of belt, knotted in front. He could never part with the rag; he did not know why, except that it was part of him: a companion, a friend, a security. He would rather have lost his fine knife than lose it, his medicine. And even as he touched it he felt that it was what tugged and strained toward the unknown south, and he felt a tingling of his fingers which spread through him till his heart thumped.

He picked up his bow and his fire stick, wrapped a generous length of caribou side ribs in the fresh skin, and called his dog.

Together they stepped out, their faces to the growing light in the south. Ahneek whined once or twice and made to turn back, testing the north with his nose. But each time he finally turned and caught up to the trudging boy.

The storm had brought remarkably little snow, since it had been mostly wind. What snow had fallen was heaped in little drifts in the lee of the patches of low shrubbery, leaving bare spaces on the more open and higher ground, the red of small willows and the patchwork color of the moss contrasting to give that mottled effect seen on the fall plumage of ptarmigan.

The land rolled slightly here, and by the time the two had crossed the third swell, fringed with its toy trees, Ahneek was content to pad easily by the side of his master's son.

CHAPTER SIX

1

Nanuk was weary. For three days now he and Ahneek had walked from long before dawn through the short fitful day, camping each night by the sliver of moon which cast a pallid light over the snow.

Today the pull of sleep came early; a pull as strong as the coastwise current which had so often lured Nook's skin boat so far along the shore that return could only be made on foot, back bent to the towline.

But now he was on a different kind of sea. A sea on edge, a sea of waves and flat waters fixed and eternal, bristled with dry and ancient growth, its darkness broken not by froth but by patches of a colder white.

The muskeg moaned and all the little stick trees shivered as if naked. Far and far they stretched in spidery webs between pool and frozen pool, channel and knoll, tussock and stone and lichened rocks where stamped and clucked the snow partridges, while all around the cotton grass danced and quivered and spread its seed on bare ground and snow alike.

At dusk Nanuk curled up in the dry, bristly tussocks and Ahneek came to his side and lay with his face to the boy's shoulder. Turning, the boy lay wide-eyed facing the sky and tried to count the stars. But more and more came out to wink at him and he sighed at the impossibility of the task; at which the big dog passed his tongue twice across those reddened eyelids, so that all the stars went out at once, and they both slept.

2

They awoke while the cold and the darkness still held the boy a little afraid; but soon Ahneek yawned, then stretched and got to his feet, his nose to the southeast, as though his own yellow eyes would bring about the birth of the sun and draw it over the black rim of the world.

Slowly the horizon paled, slowly the marish vapors of the night became first palest saffron, then pink as the flesh of an arctic salmon.

At that the boy rose too, and began to stretch the cramp from his bones. As a gesture of thanks he patted the imprint of his body in the flattened grass, picked up his caribou hide and small gear, and without a backward glance continued south through the everlasting sameness that might easily, he thought, continue to the limits of the world.

He would make no fire. It was not so bitterly cold, and having slept later than usual, he felt the need to press on.

He had been walking for some time and the sun was well up and almost in his face before he became aware of a change. And this was no change in the dreary procession of bog and drift, of tree fringe and frozen pool and gray lichen, but rather a softening of the southern horizon, as if a light film or vapor was rising and falling, half obscuring the low, red sun.

It could not be heat waves at this season, and it was not bright enough anyway; more of a smudge perhaps, a puffing thing that lived for a moment and then died.

As he paused to look, a faint southerly breeze pattered through the low shrubs and made the poolside sedges whisper as though the squat northern trolls were strumming their little harps of musk-ox wool which fluttered from the lower limbs of the scrubby spruce; and with this movement came a sweet scent, like smoke, but like no smoke of shore-cast driftwood he had ever known, yet still vaguely familiar.

The two walked on till the short day was well-nigh over, and Nanuk began to be hungry, for his breakfast had been only a scrap of meat chewed in the first hours of their walk.

They had come far, yet seemed little nearer to that strange smoke—if smoke it was. But as the light paled and the ptarmigan fell silent, Nanuk thought he sometimes saw a dull, red gleam to the south, a gleam which was not the clear and rosy afterglow of the now set sun.

By the time true darkness covered the land, by the time the first white wolf howl split the silence, the glow had increased, sometimes leaping a little, but mostly crouching behind the far distance like some skulking enemy.

The boy looked for a place to camp.

3

Nanuk had made a good breakfast before daylight. He had hoarded his supply of frozen meat, eating little and sharing the bones with Ahneek.

He had been able to augment this food with berries for which he searched where the snow was blown away or shallow. Partridge berries, his people called them, and they grew on the hummocks of the winter barrens.

Sometimes he had flushed a covey of ptarmigan and found they had been feeding on a patch, and then he had gone on his knees and filled his tea pail.

Tomorrow, he thought, as he resumed his journey, he would find such a spot and set some snares for the white birds, which were meat as good as any caribou.

Of larger game he saw little. He was evidently far ahead of the caribou. They would not be in these woods till the cold and the wind of midwinter forced them entirely from the open tundra.

It had come on to snow again, and the boy knew it would be wise to camp soon. He had started off long before dawn today. But now he was drawing so close to the red glow that he increased his pace, intent on discovering what it was that became redder and brighter as darkness fell.

Then, just beyond him, he noticed a thin spiral of smoke coming apparently out of the ground, and he turned toward it. He left the scraggy trees behind and found himself upon a large open muskeg set with small hummock. And from a crevice in this the smoke was rising. Approaching close, he saw, almost at his feet, a hole with blackened edges from which came a ruby glow, and he smelled the sweetness of burning peat, so like the smoke from tundra fires. He heard the soft hisses as the flakes of snow settled quietly and turned to steam.

Looking over to the far side of the muskeg, he could see dozens of larger craters, from all of which rose smoke which hung like mist. The glow rose and fell, until what was black became orange and turned to black again.

He stood there for a long time. As the darkness deepened before moonrise, so did the glow become brighter.

Occasionally larger, more yellow flames flared up, lighting this witches' cauldron, as tussocks of heavy grass on the face of the muskeg caught and flared. By these gusts of light, Nanuk could see the blackened trunks of small spruce; some still stood upright, others leaned grotesquely and drunkenly sideways as the slow peat fire consumed their shallow roots and burned away their footing; others were already prone.

From time to time portions of the mossy crust, underburned by the burrowing snouts of fire, fell into a crater, sending up a shower of sparks and ashes.

Aware that he was close to such a bed of ashes, aware too that the soles of his sealskin boots were becoming warm, the boy stepped back, dragging Ahneek with him. He was just in time, for at that moment a large piece of the peat he had been standing on gave way and sank about two feet with a sound like a sigh, ending in a crack as its surface vegetation, bursting into flame, momentarily illuminated the new crater.

Very slowly, inch by inch, this fire would eat its way, as it had been doing for years without number, devouring the uncounted miles of muskeg which writhed snakelike among and around the barren ridges and rocky outcrops.

He had, Nanuk knew, little to fear, so slowly did the fire probe and crawl. He could camp safely within fifty yards of the edge, and sleep in comfort, for the smoke warmed the air for many yards around. Reaching down carefully, he filled his tea pail with red embers upon which the still falling snow hissed and steamed.

CHAPTER SEVEN

1

Nanuk camped by the burning peat bog all the next day, keeping his fire replenished with chunks of the stuff which broke off around the edges of the craters. The snow let up before noon and he heard the clucking of ptarmigan off to the right. They were feeding in a patch of low berries and flew off at his approach.

He had taken the long sinew from the back of the caribou he had killed, and now he separated it into its tough threads. With these he fashioned two snare loops and set them carefully among the inch-high shrubs.

This done, and without waiting to pick any berries, he returned to his fire with a handful of leaves he had pulled from the Labrador shrubs in passing, for he was thirsty.

As he sipped the bitter but strengthening brew, he heard the ptarmigan again; but he waited an hour to give them plenty of time.

As suddenly as it had stopped, the snow began to fall again, and the wind to rise. Content to wait no longer, he returned to his snares. The birds had already left, and he could see only one, which fluttered at his approach, flapping its wings but unable to rise.

He stooped for it and quickly throttled the lovely bird with its bright eye in such dark contrast to its red comb and snowy plumage.

He found the other snare, which had failed to make a catch, and put the two in his parka. By the way the storm was rising he did not think it worthwhile to reset them, for the full-cropped birds would roost somewhere under the snow till the skies cleared.

2

The boy awoke to a cloudless sky, his body warm but heavy beneath a deep covering of snow. The short-lived storm had passed and now the moon hung low in the west. It shone with such a clear light that, except in the direction of the burning muskeg, everything stood out in strong light and shadow, the few small trees etched deeply against the sky.

Over the muskeg, however, hung a low, thick blanket of smoke, unmoving as fog above a river, obscuring it so completely that it might have been a lake, only the still visible tops of the scattered trees indicating that it was really land beneath.

All was still, from the dog at his feet to the farthest point his vision could reach; as if the world waited. Not a bird croaked, not a twig snapped, not a tree or a bush rustled. Even the moaning voice of a timber wolf would have been welcome at that breathless and lonely moment.

Nanuk shivered and rose, shaking off the clinging snow, after which he threw some wood on his peat fire, which glowed but made little flame. The wood caught and flared, breaking the silence as the dry branches crackled. Brighter now than the moon, it made all around dark except for a ruddy ring around itself. Yet the unseen, back in that darkness, now appeared not dead and still, but peopled by spirits, coming and going half seen as the light played and shadows came and went.

The boy shivered again.

He felt much colder as he filled his pail with snow and set it to boil, breaking in the Labrador bush leaves with their russet undersides, like dry leather.

He had almost half of his grilled ptarmigan left. It was the last of his food, and it was only a few mouthfuls at that, but he savored the cold meat, eating slowly.

His mind felt troubled that morning.

He had dreamed of Nook's warm tent of caribou skin, of the

flat, smiling faces, of the smell of warm bodies and cooking food and seal oil. Of the women beating the frost from the men's stiff garments, of the steam they sent forth as they dried on the racks, of the crooning of the mothers and the hunting stories of the men. He was lonely, as he had never been before. He—and the dog— alone lived in this world which frightened him by its silence or threatened him from its flitting shadows. He had heard the Shaman speak of the spirits of the trees, which were to be avoided, as Indians had to be avoided.

He almost resolved to turn back, but the land behind could harbor as many spirits as that before. He had walked many weary miles, for what? To turn back and face the barrens again? Was his spirit, his own spirit, so weak then?

No, he decided, the dice had been thrown and could not be turned another way. He must abide by their decision, as the Old Ones had always abided by the position of the ivory counters during their all-night gambling sessions.

To go back was more dangerous than to go ahead, for surely the tree belts were becoming thicker, the trees pressing closer, and in their shelter must be, somewhere, game; and where there is game there must be people, and if they could live, so could he, who was an Innuit—a preferred person.

Yet even these thoughts brought no comfort. He had no words for what he felt, but it was as though he were empty inside. Not just his belly, but under his ribs, inside his limbs, behind his eyes —all was empty. So empty that when he bowed his head and put his face in his hands only dry sobs racked him, only his shuddering shoulders told him that he was crying with unwet eyes.

He felt Ahneek come to his side, pushing under his arm with his nose, uttering little grunts of understanding, till the boy, turning, threw his arms about his companion and buried his face in the cold, frosty fur.

It was then that Ahneek licked his now wet face with his warm tongue, and with the touch Nanuk's heart again became warm, and the blood once more sang through his limbs, filling them with resolution. By the tears he knew once more that he was not an Innuit, that the life of the tents was not for him, secure though it might be.

He walked in the Sign of the Bear. He had medicine around his waist. He had feet which could take him as far as he wished! And he was not alone, for he had a companion who would be faithful unto death, a companion who felt no weak fears, who even now scratched at the snow eagerly, tongue out, ready for the venture.

Nanuk rose stiffly. He knew that never again would that weakness overcome him; that where he had been a boy he was now a man, walking erect in spirit as well as body, walking in the Sign of the Bear, the upright ancestor, ready for any challenge.

3

He cast about for his meager belongings.

They were few: the caribou skin (which could be eaten in a pinch), his precious kettle, his bow, and the few arrows for which there appeared to be little use. His father, he remembered, had a rifle; but these were hard come by and lads of his age had to use the bow. At least the bow was lighter to carry than a gun.

Hardly had the two got into their stride than a hooting came to their ears from the south. It startled them both, and they stood a moment quite still, listening. The sound came again, three, four long hollow notes, followed by a living silence.

Again and again the eerie notes sounded across the flat, bristly land.

Fear caught at Nanuk's throat. Was this one of the malignant spirits for which his new resolution was prepared? Then it had not been slow to accept the challenge, and it might even be one of the cannibal spirits of which the Innuit speak only in low voices. One of those which draw the soul from a body as it sleeps and leave it a mere mad, gibbering thing.

Nanuk quaked, but recovered himself, for a sudden thought allayed his fears. These spirits were believed in by the Innuit, therefore they existed and must be avoided by them. But he was not an Innuit, already he was sure of that, and he walked in a powerful sign. If he chose not to believe, then the thing had no power over him; for him, then, it must not exist. Everything within him told him that. Besides, the big dog seemed no longer disturbed, but was now busy digging out a vole from its runway in the moss. So the creature, or voice, or whatever it was had no power over the dog; and was he not more than a dog, he who had the power of thinking? Or did the dog think too, and had Almeck come to the same decision as himself? Wolves made a frightening noise, yet they were but wolves. He was in a strange country, so why should there not be strange creatures?

He walked on, every sense alert but not in fear now, but only curiosity.

4

His sealskin boots made little noise as he walked. But they were getting sadly worn by contact with the brittle scrub and he would have to mend them soon. In the still shallow drifts he was almost completely silent, while on the more frequent bare rocks and the windswept ridges of moss and small herbs they made only an occasional soft crunch. The dog was as noiseless, and to an onlooker the two would have seemed to be drifting vaguely, rather than marching, so silent, so almost unseen were they in that dusky half-light between the moon's setting and the sun's rising.

They added to the desolate scene, as if they themselves were mere ghosts.

They stopped again at the edge of a thicker and darker grove of swamp spruce; for once again came that hollow voice, but it was now close to them and came from overhead.

Nanuk, searching the trees with his eyes, saw a dark, shadowy form perched near the dead top of the nearest; much closer than he expected.

"Hoo, hoo," it called again and turned its great, round head, so that the boy seemed to look right into those staring yellow eyes, burning with the reflection of the first rays of light.

This surely could be no evil spirit, for evil things were invisible to any but a Shaman who had eaten strange things. An animal of some sort, he thought, when he saw its sharp ears outlined against the glow in the sky. And an animal meant meat.

For the first time since he had shot the caribou he had a use for his bow. Quickly he strung it, quicker still he adjusted an arrow and took aim.

The bowstring twanged, and just as the creature crouched—perhaps to spring?—the shaft caught it full-body. Scraping and clawing through the branches, it thudded to the ground and lay still except for the quivering of its mottled and outstretched wings. Yes, wings; for it was only a bird, though of great size; an owl, the boy guessed, for its taloned feet and round face were much like those of the white owls of the tundra; though they had not such a frightening voice.

Much cheered, he picked up the creature and moved on toward the rim of the horizon, which he could see only in bits between the trees, behind which the dawn was now glowing.

On they went, swinging far to the west to work around the smoking muskeg, always with the smoke fug on their left hand.

As the noon hour approached, Nanuk found that he could once more bear a little to the east, and by the time the sun had reached its low zenith the pall of smoke was behind his left shoulder.

The two stopped briefly, and while the boy skinned the sour-smelling bird, Ahneek resumed his mousing. With his fire drill Nanuk, sharp with hunger, kindled a blaze over which he set the owl a-broiling, carefully salvaging each drop of melting fat in his tin pail. The bird's feathers he saved, stuffing them into his seal-skin boots for added warmth. Tonight, he decided, he would patch their soles with pieces of caribou hide.

CHAPTER EIGHT

1

It was a week later, a week in which one day resembled another. A week of walking, camping, gathering berries, and snaring the now much rarer ptarmigan. A week in which, for the last two days, the boy had been reduced to cooking small portions of the lichen which grew on the more abundant outcrops. Bitter as it was, it augmented the wild tea, and had, he knew, saved many a hunter's life.

As they traveled south the snow became deeper, no longer lying in drifts but evenly spread. It puzzled Nanuk, for he had thought that the closer to the light, the less snow there might be, little knowing that the fall was heavier in the forest than on the dryer barrens. Now they were coming into bigger timber, with spruce in the hollows between the low outcrops of snow-covered rock which lay humpbacked and treeless except for gnarled birch on which the bark hung tattered. He had pulled some of this bark away and found it to be oily and easily ignited, and from then on contrived always to carry a small roll of the papery stuff in the fold of his parka for kindling his fires.

He stumbled on for two more days, looking in vain for tracks. The white hares of the barrens evidently did not venture this far. Then he came upon a little pile of cones and trash on top of the snow, from which a maze of small footprints led to the foot of a pine, the first of these trees of any size he had as yet encountered.

There came a scurrying above his head and Ahneek ran to the tree, put his front paws high against its trunk, and with his nose high, began to whine.

Nanuk, too, looked up. The scurrying came again, and then

the chattering of some small animal, while dry needles and trash
fell upon his face. Then the boy saw the cause. A little creature
with a bushy tail and a white ring about its large eyes was peering
at him, its body jerking at each sharp note. It looked like a ground
marmot of the barrens, but smaller and darker with much more
tail. Yet it was game; and soon it fell with a soft thud and lay
transfixed by a stone-tipped arrow. As it lay quivering the chat-
ter from above was repeated; and soon a second one lay with the
first.

Tucking the two into the flap of his parka and replacing the
arrows in his skin quiver, Nanuk pushed on.

2

Nanuk was soon to find that his meagre fare had considerably
weakened him. He stumbled more often and was slower to regain
his balance.

It was the next day that, walking down the slope of a smooth,
high outcrop, he felt himself slipping on the loose, shallow snow.
His feet flew out from under him and he slid at such a speed that,
despite his frantic clawing at the smooth rock, he could not regain
his feet.

He landed heavily in a deep and unseen crevice, hitting his
head hard, and lay for a moment, stunned. Then everything below
him heaved and he was thrown sideways. He became dimly aware
that Ahneek was barking and growling all at once, a thing he
rarely did. Then the dim light was blotted out, a rank sickening
scent came to his nostrils, and he felt his left arm seized between
the elbow and the shoulder. He struggled, feeling little pain but
conscious that some enormous, hairy thing was bearing him down.

He felt himself being dragged along between the steep walls of
rock; felt his cheek and nose scraped along a sharp rock. Clumsily he reached under his parka with his good arm, feeling, fum-
bling for his knife. Finally he got hold of it and stabbed upward
with all his strength, once, twice, three times. He felt the blade

drive deep and a gush of hot blood struck full in his face, almost choking him. Spitting out the salty flow, he was aware that he was in the open, at the foot of the ridge. His arm was free and he was lying on his face. All around was staccato noise, a thudding and a stamping mixed with whines and hissing growls.

Getting quickly to his feet, the boy saw a bloodstained dog holding grimly to the ear of a great, grizzled bear, which slashed at its tormentor with wide paws armed with long, cruelly curved claws. Blood was everywhere, and the bear's roaring filled the air.

3

Nanuk stooped for his knife, which now lay on the trampled snow, and as fast as he could move on his bruised and trembling legs, struggled back to where his whalebone bow should be. But it was smashed beyond repair, and only one arrow lay unbroken. Hardly knowing what he was doing, he stooped for a heavy stone which lay loose at the mouth of the crevice.

Staggering under its weight, he approached the two animals, now silent but for their hoarse breathing; the blood from the bear's throat dripping steadily, turning the snow to crimson mush beneath them. Desperately the beast lashed out at its tormentor, while the dog dodged this way and that without losing his hold. Stepping close as Ahneek dragged the bear's heavy head sideways, the boy brought down the stone with all his might on the creature's piglike snout. The bear roared and shook his head, blood now gushing from its broken jaw, almost shaking off the grip that Ahneek still held on its tattered ear.

Now, with heaving flanks, the bear gave one more desperate lunge and its ear tore free from the dog's teeth.

Turning from the dog, it now made for Nanuk, who was clambering up the rocks. The bear followed, but he was weakening and sluggish from the loss of the blood which now matted his foreparts and belly. So it was that the boy was able to scramble high enough to avoid the blow aimed at him by the wickedly spiked paw. The dog rushed in again, covering himself in blood as he seized the bear by the great tendon above the hairy hind foot. The bear turned, and round and round they went like a whirlpool in some red rapids, the dog avoiding those awful front paws, the bear's head sagging lower and lower.

Nanuk, who had gained the crest of the outcrop, now felt such a stab of pain in his left arm that he looked quickly at it. His parka of heavy caribou hide, hair outward, was mashed and punctured and blood was running down into his mitt.

It could wait, he thought; it must wait.

Only assuring himself that the limb was not broken, he grasped the knife more firmly and began to descend to the ghastly arena below with some idea of using his weapon again. Arriving at the bottom, he stepped around the circling combatants, looking for an opening. He knew he must help Ahneek as the dog had helped him. He was about to chance a quick stab at the creature's flank, when quite suddenly the bear's limbs sagged and it fell sideways, its head striking the snow with a thud. The hoarse breathing had become a bubbling in its throat, and even that soon ceased. Only then, when the last shudder had passed over the steaming body, did Ahneek let go of the tendon, stagger away from the bear, and fall on his side.

4

Limping over to the faithful dog, Nanuk knelt. Putting his good arm under the heavy, blood-matted head, he raised it up. Ahneek whined feebly with pleasure and tried to wag his tail. Gently the boy scrutinized the dog's flanks, back, and belly. Mercifully the belly had not been slashed open as he feared. But there were deep claw slashes along Ahneek's ribs and flanks and one hind foot had lost two toes and was even now swelling, and when he touched it Ahneek trembled and whimpered.

Turning over the dog's heavy body was not easy with one arm

but the boy accomplished it, and found to his relief that the dog's other side bore only a couple of superficial cuts. Lifting its head again, he raked snow beneath it with one foot, so that it no longer lay flat.

Going back to the rocks, he found that his stiffness was wearing off and the pain of his arm speeded rather than slowed him. There Nanuk gathered in one arm his arrows, both the sound and the broken, as well as the hide, and returned. The arrows he put aside for the present; later he would have to make shafts for the heads from the broken ones. Now he unrolled the caribou hide by Ahneek and managed to drag him onto it, again packing snow on one side so that he lay naturally and comfortably.

CHAPTER NINE

1

It was now absolutely necessary for Nanuk to get a fire going. Already cooling off from his exertions, he realized the danger of frostbite in his wounded arm and face.

Making the fire was a slow and painful process, for while he could use his wounded arm a little, he had not sufficient strength in it to press heavily enough on the upright stick while he operated the bow with his good arm. After several attempts he found that he had to put the full weight of his throbbing head on top of his hand, and then press with all his might.

The new bow was clumsy, too; the string kept slipping and had to be tightened with fingers weak from the numbing cold, for much snow as well as blood had got into his mitts.

Finally, however, a little puff of smoke rose and the punkwood glowed, and he was able to coax his little shreds of birch bark into flame.

He held his breath as he laboriously piled dead twigs and watched them catch, followed by chunks of resinous branches. Only when the blaze shot high did he realize how close to panic he had been in those last moments. Now, at last, he could warm his hands and dry his wet mitts.

But he did not enjoy that warm glow for long, for he had to turn his attention to the dead bear before it froze beyond possibility of skinning. He wanted that skin, and he needed some meat.

2

He noticed that the monster—a brown bear of the tundra—was singed almost to the skin along its belly and about its paws, and above its carnivorous stench his nose could discern the faint odor with which he was now so familiar, the scent of burning peat.

He guessed that the beast had been denned-in on the muskeg, no doubt at the edge of some higher ground; and that the fire had surrounded it and edged close enough to disturb it and cause it to vacate its den, for it would not as yet be in full sleep. In escaping from the danger it must have been obliged to cross a crater full of still glowing ashes, or perhaps more than one.

Angry and sullen, the bear must have wandered looking for some safer spot in which to resume its interrupted rest; never stopping till it came to the crevice, many miles from the fire. Here it had denned, the new snow which had covered its tracks also serving to cover it with a warm blanket. Even the burning muskeg had been far south for a barren-land bear to stray; but strange things happen, and birds and beasts are where you find them.

The boy would have to deal with the animal now, before his arm stiffened beyond use. He was weary to the bone and his gashed nose and cheek were sore and bloody, but he set his teeth and drove his knife (that wonderful knife which like a live thing had found the bear's jugular) through the tough skin just behind the heel, and then, blade up, cut along the hind leg to the tail and along the great backbone, over the shoulder and back along the flank, avoiding the scorched belly, and so to the starting point. It would be but half a hide or less, he thought, as he began to peel it back, cutting away at the stringy tissues; but he could never turn over that dead weight to get at the other side. Nevertheless, it would still make a fine robe to lie on if he could manage to carry it.

If only Ahneek were well and strong!

Pulling the last of the hide away, he turned to the dog and could have shouted for joy to see that Ahneek was sitting up and licking his flank. Perhaps he would live! A surge of joy flowed through Nanuk.

In spite of the throbbing pain of his arm he felt the better for his exertions. They had somehow calmed him and he felt in control of circumstances again.

He hummed a little as he stretched the hide flat, close enough to the fire to prevent it freezing.

3

He continued to hum happily as he cut long slices from the bear's rump, first removing the two-inch layer of fat which covered the red meat. Both meat and fat he sliced into smaller pieces, which he laid on the snow to freeze. He would have a good supply for the next few days, but a supply limited by what he could carry.

As he set two pieces to broil for his supper, his thoughts revolved around his lucky escape. Truly, he walked in the Sign of the Bear, the great beast which the tribes held in such reverence, even though they killed them. But it was the bear which had died, not he, for the beast of the cave could not withstand his spirit. Or was it really *his* spirit? The Innuits spoke always of bad spirits which dwelt unseen, outside the body, evil spirits which if not appeased could destroy the spirit of man. But might there not be one great, all-powerful Good Spirit, mightier than they, who protected people, who gave meat in due season, who gave to man the power to overcome? He knew the owl had, after all, been no evil spirit. And he felt no presence of evil in these woods. The friendly trees gave fuel, the Labrador herb gave him drink, the bear would give him meat, hide, and sinew. Why, he thought, should people fear the unknown? Or was it that if one walked through fear, then fear had no power?

How he wished there was some wise one who could teach him

these things. How he wished the Good Spirit could, would speak
to him! Perhaps someday he would know. Perhaps the Good
Spirit even now *was* speaking, through his own mind. . . . Perhaps he would find the answer at his journey's end.

It was long since dark, with an overcast sky, but the firelight
cast a ruddy circle of light which struck the trunks of the nearest
spruce trees, turning them to bright copper.

He would eat now, he thought, and feed Ahneek, though there
was still much to do before he could rest.

4

His meal over, the flavor of bear rank in his mouth, Nanuk
rose. Ahneek, full fed, was lying comfortably, snoring a little. They
would both be stiff by morning; perhaps not able to travel. But
they had fire and they had meat—there was no hurry, the south
would still be the south.

It was getting much colder, and he made a rough shelter of
forked sticks and spruce boughs, open to the fire's warmth, and
laid down his caribou hide, now roughly tanned from use, upon
a few spruce fronds.

From the comparative comfort of this shelter he now turned
to the important matter of his wound and Ahneek's injuries.

As he considered what best to do, a resinous piece of deadfall
blazed up, the gum burning and sputtering madly as it melted;
and with that the boy remembered how wounds had been treated
in the place of tents.

The women used this very spruce gum; one of the things they
sometimes brought back when the band hunted far to the south
where the little trees grew.

Nanuk rose and went toward the trees, whose lower trunks
blushed in the light of the flames while their dark tops were lost
in the indigo sky.

Several large globules of the balm hung, hard and granulated,
from gashes about the height of his shoulder, made by a caribou

rubbing its antlers. With his knife he pried off several lumps and returned to his shelter, holding a piece of resin toward the heat on his knife blade. When it began to drip like honey, he laid knife and all on a piece of bark, painfully stripped off his parka, and examined his wounds.

He was surprised that they were not deeper, for although his whole upper arm was now the greenish color of an eider duck's egg, the tooth marks did not appear to be deep. Caribou hair, forced through his parka, made a bloody mat which had stopped the bleeding. He first thought of removing this crust, but finally decided to leave well enough alone. He remembered that the old women never touched a wound with water. This, they said, drove the poison in, and it should come out.

He dabbed the whole area with the sticky gum, hoping he was doing the right thing. He had, he thought, seen worse wounds than this heal rapidly, and he took it for a good sign that his arm felt hot and feverish.

Replacing his parka, leaving his left arm out of the sleeve and bound to his body with his medicine rag, he next turned his attention to the dog, who was lying head to flank, his nose covered by his bushy tail.

Carefully he plastered the worst of Ahneek's wounds with the gum, but lightly, for he knew the dog's own tongue would be the best medicine; that, and food and rest.

Dead tired, his eyes red rimmed, the boy threw big chunks of damp deadfall on the fire, banked it up with ashes, pulled his parka hood up and the bear hide over him, and fell asleep.

CHAPTER TEN

1

He woke within an hour. A great gust of nausea seized him, then another, and he had to rise and go to one side, bent over

At last relief came as he emptied his meal on the snow. Again and again he vomited, his mouth bitter and stinking. Perhaps he had eaten too greedily of the bear meat before it had properly cooled, he thought, or was it poison from his wound which caused this rebellion of his stomach?

At last, exhausted, he returned to his bed and fell into dreamless sleep.

It was long past his usual time for rising when Nanuk awoke. He was aware that ravens were croaking almost in his ear.

Sitting up, he saw two of them picking at the carcass of the bear, while another was walking with rolling gait and sly eye toward his store of cut meat. Seizing a stick from his pile of firewood, the still sleepy boy threw it toward the black scavengers, which took wing and, after circling, lit, each one separately, in the tops of some scattered trees, croaking back and forth and wiping their soiled beaks on the knotty boughs, their plumage burnished by the risen sun.

Nanuk drew the ashes of his fire together, blew for a moment on some red coals, and built it up. For all his weakness he now felt clearheaded, as he set his snow-filled pail over the flames. As soon as the snow melted he dropped in some small pieces of meat to boil.

He knew he must be careful of what he ate now; he would take a little soup only, gradually increasing the amount of meat till he could stomach solids.

Ahneek got up painfully and limped across to a tree where he left his sign clumsily, then returned to sit by the boy, nuzzling him with his nose. The meat did not seem to have affected the dog; on the contrary he seemed much stronger and when a wolf howled in the far distance he got to his feet, hackles up, and gave vent to a deep growl.

The boy quieted him. He hoped the wolves would not scent the kill.

Having taken sparingly of the hot broth, Nanuk laid himself down again, the dog at his side.

So they dozed and rested while the pale sun, half seen through the frost fog, ran his short course.

2

Toward morning his sleep became far from dreamless. He tossed this way and that. He thought he woke once or twice, yet he was in a no man's land and could not be sure. Strange visions danced and gibbered before his eyes. Balls of fire came between him and something for which he seemed to search on hands and knees.

Voices, too, spoke to him from trees—always little trees—which danced a jig in and out among the rocks. Something roared and smothered him and he tried to raise a feeble arm; but the arm was hot, puffed, full of knives, and it would not obey. Huge ravens jeered at him from swinging, dancing trees. He could smell the carrion on their horny bills.

Then he was walking, walking, but he could not feel his feet and he kept stumbling. . . .

3

Nanuk had lost all track of time when he came to. It was dark and very cold. The fire had apparently burned out. Ahneek was standing over him, rumbling deep in his throat. The boy half turned and flung up his good arm as if to ward off danger. The dog stooped and licked his face, then resumed his stance, staring into the velvety blackness.

With a clear head but pitifully weak, the boy crawled to the fire. Painfully he reached beneath his parka and found a piece of birch bark which he coaxed into flame from some few embers which lay deep in the ashes. Quickly he fed it with small twigs broken from his store of branches.

As the small fire caught, he heard a muffled movement from the darkness beyond the faint outline of the bear carcass. Then he saw a pair of yellow eyes; and another. Ahneek made a stiff jump forward on three legs and let out a growl which was more like a roar.

The eyes disappeared like a flame blown out.

So, the wolves had found the kill. It was not a good thought. Wolves were cowards, but a weak man and a crippled dog . . . ?

He replenished his fire, and when the sticks had caught, he threw a branch with what strength he could in the direction of the wolves, sparks flying in an arc.

All was quiet now, and it was not long before the two heard a howl from at least a mile away, answered by another, and yet another; all from different quarters.

They were safe for the time being, and if he kept the fire going well, he felt they would still be for as long as they needed to stay. A few days would give them both strength to continue on their way; after which the wolves would be welcome to the mutilated carcass.

He drank more soup and essayed to chew a morsel of boiled meat from which he had pared the fat.

4

The travelers stayed over a week in the snug camp between the humped rock and the sheltering spruce. During that time

Ahneek occupied himself for hours in licking his wounds, which looked pink and healthy. Nanuk's arm swelled horribly and smelled bad, and he had a sore lump in his left armpit; but he knew nothing of blood poisoning and so accepted the discomfort cheerfully enough.

On the fifth day he removed his parka by the warmth of the fire and took his arm from the band. He started to lay more gum on the swollen wound but Ahneek pushed aside his hand and began to lick the encrusted scab. Nanuk lay back, for the feel of that pink tongue was soothing.

Several crusts loosened and dropped away, and at one extra energetic lick, matter began to ooze. As more of the creamy yellow stuff exuded, the boy wiped it off with a handful of dry moss.

Nanuk felt much relieved, and replaced the parka, but this time let the arm hang loose inside it. Thereafter he would expose his arm daily to his friend's healing tongue.

Daily he increased the amount of food which he took. Daily he had to stumble among the trees in the bitter cold, to gather twigs and dry limbs, or kick about for deadfall in the snow. Fire was life now, and each day he had to wander farther afield on this quest for fuel, and each day he felt his strength increasing.

The day before leaving the camp Nanuk went over to the carcass, now partly riddled and plentifully whitewashed by the ravens. He wanted something to remember it all by; something to show should he ever have to tell the story. With his knife he cut off all the great crescent-shaped claws from the beast's front feet. Then he thought of knocking out a tooth or two from between the rubbery lips, now drawn back from the gums.

It was then, looking at the yellow, blunted incisors and at the gaps in the jaw, that he realized this was an old, perhaps a very old beast.

He saw, too, that its sunken eyes had been running matter, whether as the result of smoke and hot ashes or some other injury he did not know. He realized that it was due to these facts that he had escaped with no worse wound than that which (he felt sure) was now fast healing.

Had he known it, it was because the bear had eaten no meat for many weeks and its passage through the ashes had effectively sterilized its claws that there had not been far worse poisoning of his wound and the dog's.

Before he lay down, he inspected his arm and found that the swelling had subsided, the edges of the punctures were roughening, and new pink skin was slowly spreading. He felt a great sense of thankfulness to the Unseen Power which worked even as he slept.

5

Nanuk made careful preparations for continuing his journey. Not yet back to his full strength, he nevertheless felt happy and completely assured, in spite of the still bitter cold. First he made a new fire drill, choosing his material carefully and this time carving a roughly circular piece of sound deadfall for a handle with which to hold down the rotator, twisting his knife in the underside to make a hollow so it would not slip. These pieces he put in his parka fold.

Then he mended the arm of his torn parka with some lengths of sinew, piercing holes with his knife point and using a small piece of his caribou hide for a patch.

He also dried out his sweat-dampened boots, hanging them well above the fire on long sticks, and while they hung, dried and fluffed out the owl feathers before replacing them.

Slowly and methodically he busied himself, preparing for every eventuality he might have to meet; even to drying out a double handful of moss to take with him should he have to camp where none was available.

He wanted to take the piece of bear hide and cast about in his mind how best to do this.

The thing was partly frozen, so he thawed it by the fire, then scraped off as much fat and tissue as he could; after which he worked and rubbed it with his feet to break down the fiber.

When he had finished it was hardly tanned, but it was at least more pliable than it had been, and he knew that with use it would improve.

He wished he could pack it on Ahneek, wrapped around some meat, but the dog was still carrying one hind foot and he dismissed the thought.

He thought of a sledge; but with no drill to make holes for lashing, he dismissed that also.

He compromised by first cutting a long, narrow strip from one side of the piece of hide. He then wrapped up a good store of sliced and frozen meat which clinked like stones, folding the hide over and over. With the strip he bound the pack together, leaving two long ends to put over his shoulders and tie at the back, making several adjustments before the pack sat comfortably on his shoulders.

When satisfied, he replaced the knife carefully in the rag next to his skin, picked up his crude bow and his arrows, and started with never a backward glance, Ahneek limping at his heels.

CHAPTER ELEVEN

1

They did not go far that day. They had started late and the boy tired easily. What was worse, they came to a short but steep bank above a river which crossed their path from southwest to northeast. From the left a roaring sound came to them, a sound which was new. Had he been able to see around a bend half a mile in that direction, the boy would have seen a seething rapid, the source of the noise; but he could not, and he looked up, thinking a great wind had risen. But the treetops along the bank were perfectly still, swathed in white frost which had gathered on them as the waters below had steamed in the cold before they finally froze. He judged by this that the ice would be none too thick.

The two made their way to the water's edge, Nanuk impeded by the heavy pack and the now much deeper snow which made progress difficult, as it hid the holes and small rocks.

They camped in the shelter of an overhanging bank; Nanuk followed the routine of first starting a fire, then gathering enough wood to last till morning, then cooking and eating. After caching supplies high up in a tree where they would be safe from marauders, he banked the fire and settled down for the night, sharing Ahneek's warmth on a bed of spruce boughs.

2

A mass of pink fog was rising beyond the bend, and a few fine wisps hung over the ice before them.

The two stood in the pale morning light, once more at the river's edge. Nanuk took a long pole to test the ice ahead as he stepped out for the opposite shore, a hundred yards ahead. There was little snow on the ice and walking was easy, for evidently the strength of the current had prevented freezing until the last really cold days. As they reached the middle of the channel the boy felt the ice bend beneath him, and at that moment saw the narrow open channel before them, the dark water rushing northward, a slight fog hovering above. They both stopped, then turned back, the ice giving way behind them. For a moment Nanuk thought they would go through and held his pole before him parallel to the ice, to hold him up if they did.

But the moment passed and they were soon on firm ice again.

The boy was sweating now. He turned southwest at the shore and together they followed the loops and bends, looking for a safe crossing, but could find none and as the moon was rising later now, they camped shortly after dusk.

3

That night the frost strengthened. So bitter was it that Nanuk built two fires a few feet apart. As they lay, the two could hear the trees above the bank popping like rifle shots, while the ice below boomed and muttered.

They slept fitfully and awoke chilled. Little crystals of ice clung to the boy's eyelashes and to the young down of his cheeks and lip. His parka hood was heavily rimed and so were Ahneek's jowls.

Had he been still among the Innuits, he thought, now would be the time to start plucking out those hairs with a pair of clamshell tweezers.

Thinking things over, Nanuk now decided to continue down the west bank of the river until the increasing cold completely and safely froze the ice to bearing point. He would be working a little west; indeed if the river curved much more to the right he would almost be forced to cross soon, but as it flowed now he would at least be making his way south.

For two more days they pushed on, and each night the howling of the wolves, which had found the bear carcass, sounded fainter until it could no longer be heard. Sometimes for a mile or more they could follow a smooth shore line where walking was easy, but in other places they had to clamber painfully over rocks and fallen trees, or even climb the bank and thread their way through the brush and timber.

It was clear and sharply cold, and the steam from their breath hung like smoke in their wake. There was no warmth in the sun, but it raised their spirits to see it rise; and as it hung low in the south, the black shadows of the forest and the bank fled, to be replaced by narrow ribbons of blue shadow running over the hummocky snow from the base of every tree.

No squirrels chattered now, for they were deep in their big nests high in the spruce. The boy looked for tracks but found none. The snow was unbroken for mile on mile.

The nights were even colder, but they had their fires; and lying in their tiny world warmed by its glow, the two cared little for the black fathomless depths around; while overhead the sky was so charged with brilliant stars that it made a bright canopy above the somber tops of spruce.

On the last night the stars were dimmed by the pale green and pink of the northern lights which played and swung sometimes so close that Nanuk felt he could touch their trembling curtains with his fingertips; but they always retreated back to their ice palace beyond the northern rim.

The boy knew this as a sign for some letup in the bitter, harsh cold; and next morning, to be sure, the frost eased. In that frozen wilderness a rise of but a few degrees comes as a relief, and the two companions broke camp and stepped forth almost gaily, trotting from time to time like children, Ahneek snatching at the snow with his jaws and throwing it up to sparkle like a shower of diamonds.

4

So they traveled, enthralled by the beauty of the morning. The snow swathed the trees, which stood pure and unsullied against a cobalt sky shot with a few fleecy clouds, gold and faintly pink. Only the river below was half obscured, for over it hung a film of frost-fog, blue-gray beneath the shadowing banks.

Rising at dawn, they had twice heard the solemn hoots of an owl; but as the sun strengthened it fell silent, and search the snow-burdened trees as he might, Nanuk could not locate the bird. He would be glad of any game now, for the bear meat was running out.

But because he had never heard of compasses and maps, of guided tours and comfortable hotels, the boy was as sure of his directions as a horse heading back for his home range, as wildfowl seeking the sun, as a pipit returning to its nest on the sameness of the tundra.

When he had the sun to guide him, he used it; when skies were leaden he knew the south by the lie of the snowdrifts, by the trees' lighter south and darker north sides. In the predawn darkness and after sunset he had the stars and the moon, and when these were obscured his instinct held him on his course.

Never having been frightened by tales of failure, he hardly thought of it. Accidents, yes; he had seen them—the overturned skin boat; drownings in icy waters; broken bones from falls—all these he knew, but they were not failures. They were merely the hazards of life for both man and beast.

CHAPTER TWELVE

1

The crossing Nanuk chose was about forty-five miles upstream from where he had first met the northward-flowing river. He looked across and realized that it was considerably narrower here, the banks less high and more heavily clothed with willows. He heard no roar of rapids and no fog hung above the ice, on which the snow lay deep and untrodden. He scraped a small patch of ice clean and, looking down, could see no flow of dark water beneath. All was opaque and even the rocks were frozen firmly to the bottom.

He knew such ice could carry a herd of caribou and as he started confidently across he realized that his former attempt had been thwarted by shallow rapids, reluctant to freeze.

Walking in the much deeper snow, he knew he would soon have to contrive some snowshoes, or as more snow came he would eventually find himself floundering helplessly. For in spite of the unaccustomed sun at such a season, he knew it was near mid-winter; and the heaviest snowfalls were ahead.

2

They stopped for a moment on the far side, looking back; the dog pressed close to the boy's side.

Now their tracks made blue slots across the snowy channel; and the crossing seemed an achievement, a marker on their journey.

Satisfied, they climbed the bank together.

Passing through the heavy fringe of timber bordering the water-way, they came to more open ground again, where the drifts were deeper; and it was here the boy saw a dozen sagging poles set in a circle with their tops meeting.

Excited, Nanuk plunged forward. He knew it for the pole frame of a hunter's camp, for his own people sometimes used the same pattern, covering the poles with skins; although their summer lodges were more often oblong.

He kicked the snow away and found long-dead ashes. No one had been here recently. The lodge must have been put up by In-dians, he thought, and resolved to proceed with caution, for he must now be within the hunting ground of the savage and uncer-tain tribes which had no love for Innuits, and he had no wish to be taken by surprise.

Leaving the denuded wigwam, he walked straight for the south, passing several more sets of lodge poles, some partially collapsed; and it was a much greater surprise when he suddenly came upon a small log shack. He had never seen one before, but he recog-nized it as man's work by the trimmed logs and the cut poles of the roof, covered, he later found, with earth from a borrow-pit into which he nearly fell. Some weeds grew on the roof as he could see by the sere and brittle fronds which shivered above the snow covering. A round black thing like a piece of small log stood up near the roof's center.

There were no tracks, but the faint trace of a path, little more than an opening between the thick growth of willows at the back, tempted him to follow it; and doing so, he found that beyond the brush lay a small, deep creek. He could hear water gurgling be-neath the snow and ice.

Whoever had once occupied the cabin must have obtained his water from this little stream which obviously ran into the river he had lately crossed.

3

The cabin door was ajar, and the rising wind made it creak on its rawhide hinges.

Nanuk entered, looking carefully about.

There was just enough light for him to make out a rough table of poles, a bunk of the same—although he had no idea what it was—and a rusty tin stove of the folding type. This he recognized, for he had seen one or two of these among the Innuits.

"Here we stop," he said aloud to Ahneek and began to gather twigs. An armful of split wood already lay sprawled on the dirt floor.

He had some difficulty with his fire. He had to start it on the floor, for he could not work his drill within the narrow stove which was fed from the front. He was obliged to lift the burning piece between two twigs to get it through the small square door.

After two failures in which his tiny fire shattered in his too eager hands, and all but went out, he finally succeeded, and smoke was soon pouring from the pipe on the roof. How he wished then that he had a flint-and-steel tinderbox such as Nook and some of the other Innuits possessed.

The only other thing in the cabin was a handleless lard pail, much blackened. This was a real find and he used it to boil up a stew of bear meat while his own small tea pail reverted to its original function, but this time he made a brew of spruce tips.

He had never seen or heard of this drink, but instinctively guessed, from chewing a little, that spruce should not be poisonous; nor did he know that this was just what his blood required to remove the last traces of poison from his system.

He drank only a little of it, however, sipping it slowly till his body glowed with warmth.

Long before they bedded down the sun had set, and the late moon, shining through the rawhide window, touched with silver the two who slept so soundly on the floor.

4

The morning after their arrival at the cabin the dawn broke feverishly. To either side of the sun itself two attendant "dogs" glowed like smoky candles, while liverish wisps of cloud scudded across the sky, foretelling high winds.

And even more bitter cold. The air became more and more foggy, more full of ice crystal, and soon the horizon became obscured.

By evening the snow was coming in gusts, lashing around the cabin, writhing snakelike across the open ground.

Nanuk felt that this was the time to make some kind of snowshoes. Although his arm was getting stronger, both it and he would be better for a rest under cover.

The days were short, and he doubted that he could do what he wanted in less than two or even three.

While waiting for it to be light enough to work in the cabin, he occupied himself in searching outside for a good supply of fuel, gathering large dry limbs and fallen, half-buried pieces from among the trees.

Then for his proposed work he had to look for spruce boughs which were sound but not too stiff, and cut them to length for the side bows, two to each shoe. These he had to steam at the front ends, so as to give the toes the proper upward bend, without which they would catch on every obstruction. He notched these ends to make a sitting for the sinew he would use to bind them together. The hind ends he pared down so that they would fit snugly to form a long heel.

He had tried to bend a limb right around to make the rounded point and circular shape he was familiar with among his own people; but the limb had splintered, and this obliged him to use two side bows.

With his knife he leveled the top and bottom sides and slotted the bows to let in the crossbars. His first bars were too long and he saw that to force the bows apart with them would not do, so he finally shortened them to about nine inches Having inserted them, he then drew the fronts together, lacing them tightly with straps of hide wound round as he had seen his father do. The test now would be whether he could bend them enough to join the heels. Slowly and steadily he tightened the sinews he had looped around them till, without cracking, they came together. Lashing them tight, he looked for some way to drill holes for the final fastening.

His fire drill would do if he only had a point which would pierce through wood. He tried an arrowhead but it broke. Then, searching, he found a short thing of metal driven in the log wall. It was a nail, but he had never seen one before. It took him some time to draw it from the wall, but finally he succeeded and saw it was sharp enough for his purpose. Not to sacrifice his good drill, he cut another short length of round stick which he carefully split at one end so as to insert his point, which he bound fast. With his bow to rotate the thing, he made the required holes at intervals all around the wooden bows. Through these holes he would later thread the laces he had prepared for the webbing. These were all cut in thin strips from the caribou hide and he left them to soak overnight in water in order to become soft and easily stretched. It was dark when he got thus far. Enough for today, he thought. The frames were made and the lashings cut. He boiled and ate a little meat and spread the bear hide for a cover.

Laboriously, for his arm was hurting, he spent most of the next day weaving the webs and the strong wrapping which held the bars from spreading, leaving plenty of room in the center for the toes of his footwear, which would have to pass between them.

He finished by rubbing some bear fat into the rawhide, and set the two somewhat crooked and ill-matched snowshoes to dry, which would tighten up the webs and lashings.

CHAPTER THIRTEEN

1

The two days' delay had strengthened both of them. Yet because of the glare of the sun-dazzled snow they were traversing, and the work he had been engaged in by the dull light of the cabin, Nanuk's eyes felt sore and throbbing. Today the overcast sky had cleared again and he knew that the landscape would be bright. Remembering how the Innuit hunters had overcome the hazard of snow blindness, he took time in the early morning to carve himself a pair of eye goggles from a piece of sound birch bark, leaving mere slits for his eyes and attaching to each side a rawhide string from his dwindling caribou hide, with which to bind them on.

This work he did by the glow of light from the front of the little stove, his eyes streaming from the smoke.

Ahneek could now put his lame foot to the ground with only a suggestion of a limp; and the boy, seeing this, decided that the big dog was able to carry the pack.

This he lashed to the dog's back with the binding piece, passing an end across his chest to prevent the (now light) load of meat from slipping back and possibly turning under his belly.

They started out, looking now like a respectable snowshoed hunter and his well-packed dog rather than a pair of ill-equipped wanderers.

2

Daily now the forest thickened. The barrens and the land of little sticks were becoming no more than a memory brought to mind by the occurrence of occasional open muskegs.

They were in the heart of the taiga, the boreal forest. Even the muskegs showed patches of arctic birch and red willows only half covered by the deep snow. Once they saw a tiny owl sitting on one of the twigs. Nanuk could have taken it in his hand, but it was too small to eat and he passed it by with a smile because it looked so comical as it turned its round head toward him.

Once it snowed all through a windless day, shutting off the distance like a blanket and muffling all sound. It felt much warmer, but Nanuk was not deceived; he knew that when the sky cleared it would be colder than ever, though the days seemed to be slowly lengthening.

In the shelter of the timber the white flakes drifted slowly down; where they reached the ground they added to the already deep white cover, but elsewhere they once again blanketed the trees that had so recently been relieved of their burden by the wind.

The best walking was still in the shade of the larger trees where the snow was less deep, but in the old burned-over ground, where only a few scattered and blasted trees still remained upright, the going was hard, for here the logs lay crisscross under great mounds of snow, and he had to go carefully, and step from one to the other, always making sure to plant each foot with its instep squarely on a log—otherwise he would have broken his hard-won snowshoes.

3

Two days later they came to a low swamp area where the black spruce were only a foot or so higher than himself and grew almost as thick as rushes.

They looked like little peaks of snow, their limbs hidden and tops bent down. There was no apparent room for passage between, but the little forest stretched as far as he could see on both sides, so he pushed into it, his shoulders and head brushing the burdened fronds from which lumps of snow cascaded over him. All among the dwarf trees was a dense growth of the Labrador shrub, which sometimes tangled in the mesh of his shoes as he tramped over them.

The swamp was only half a mile wide, yet he was much relieved to strike higher ground beyond. He stopped a moment to adjust the dog's pack and, looking back, could easily follow his trail by eye, for through the mass of snow-plumed spruce it made a dark line of exposed branches.

Every night the boy searched for a good camping place on higher ground where large spruce grew and spread wide their needled and cone-heavy limbs; for under these it was easier to find firewood and the shallow snow could be scraped away to expose the soft duff of old and rotted needles upon which he could make a comfortable bed.

He was able to kill a squirrel or two during these few milder days, and once a big black and white woodpecker with a red crest which yakked at him from a dead tree.

Otherwise he saw little signs of life beyond the remains of an old wolf kill from which an ermine scuttled. From the shape of its bones he was able to tell that it must have been a caribou, and he felt heartened, for he had not seen a sign of those animals since his journey began.

4

They traveled for another month, while the woods became denser. Now he began to see man sign. Here some cut stumps indicated a camping place. There a blazed tree showed where a lynx-pen deadfall now rotted. Some human hand had made the pen of upright twigs, baited at the closed end to lure the cat within. When it seized the bait, the heavy log would be released, which would break its back.

His supply of bear meat was long exhausted, and for many days now he had seen no ptarmigan. He had made do with squirrels and with lichens from the rocks, but there was little nourishment in them. He little knew it but now he was far south of the winter pastures of the little northern deer, for which he looked in vain.

Several times, however, he came across tracks, but they were old and covered by new snow. Then one morning he came to an open muskeg and saw five animals watching him. Even at a distance of perhaps three hundred yards he could see how fine and fat these caribou were.

They were the larger woodland caribou but they had recently lost three of their little band to the dark Chipewyans, and were restless. After snorting and stamping they wheeled and made off in a flurry of kicked-up snow; and were soon lost to sight in the timber.

The sun reached a little higher each day now, and after another cold snap in the middle of February there came a change, and following a light, soft breeze the snow began to glaze in the open.

Lumps of soft snow began to fall from the trees and the squirrels could be heard chattering to each other from tree to tree, while their little feeding places below were packed down with their tracks. Nanuk shot several with his bow, but he longed for something less stringy and sharp to the tongue.

More and more broad-leaved trees began to appear—now in their winter nakedness. First in scattered twos and threes, then in stands between the clumps of spruce. Many open, grassy muskegs wound through the forest, threaded by small unseen creeks, their sluggish brown waters frozen solid. In places, beds of cattails followed these narrow channels, their shivering spear-pointed tops making pale ocher patches.

In one such opening the boy heard a series of clucking sounds and saw, among the poplars at its edge, several large brownish-gray birds, the shape of ptarmigan but larger. They were climbing among the topmost twigs, reaching this way and that for buds which they swallowed with straining throats.

He was able to get close enough to shoot one with an arrow but before he could loose another (for he had long since mended the broken ones) the covey whirred away, clucking loudly and scattering the white frost from the twigs among which they swerved and dodged. He wondered what name they might have, these fine birds which are known to whites as sharp-tailed grouse.

5

Twice he crossed the tracks of some big beasts which must have had longer legs than caribou, for though they sank much further in the deep snow they seemed not to flounder; and he found places among the willows and alders where one had been browsing on twigs well above Nanuk's head, and on whose snags hung tufts of coarse hair, almost black. Here also were piles of dung like hard cones, of a yellow color, not black like a caribou's.

Whatever they were, they did not go in herds, for each animal apparently lived by itself.

Nanuk also killed several strange birds from among a group squatting among the spruce overhead.

They were much darker than the brown one he had shot in the poplars, and they sat and peered at him, stretching out their necks.

The first one he pierced with an arrow fell with a thud and a flutter, but the others did not take flight; they only stretched their necks further as they contemplated the fall of their comrade. He downed another and still the rest only clucked and shifted their feet, making no move to fly. He got two more and then missed the fifth shot, the arrow striking the hard branch and falling to earth. As though disappointed that the show was over, the remaining three now launched themselves on short, rounded wings and disappeared into the gloom of the forest, flying right through the thickset branches yet not striking them.

The boy picked up his game. They too, like the brown bud-eaters, had feathered legs, but when he later dressed them he found in their crops no tasty berries or aromatic buds for his delight, but only dry spruce needles; and their flesh was flavored to bitterness with the same.

It was much later that he found they were called "fool hens" and he could understand why.

6

What Nanuk first took to be dead spruce scattered through the meadows now, with milder weather, began to take on a strange purplish tint on their smaller twigs. They grew straight like spruce, and their limbs, leaving the trunk in whorls, grew parallel to the ground, but in place of needles the branches were spotted with little budlike swellings. Evidently their needles had dropped, yet the twigs were lissom. No dead tree was like that and Nanuk was puzzled.

Leaving the tamaracks, he went on, and began to see armfuls of twigs and small branches in the larger trees. But not until he saw the sinister outline of a round, sharp-eared head looking at him from over the rim of one of these did he realize that these were birds' nests. He thought they must have been made by the owls themselves; for the big hawks responsible for these high architectural efforts would not return to these woods until the opening of the buds.

Nanuk was fascinated by all he saw. Indeed the Strong Woods did not disappoint him, and as he walked he contrasted the mass of line and color with the harsh and brittle austerity of his old home on the barrens.

CHAPTER FOURTEEN

1

A few days later they crossed an old toboggan trail. The two followed it a short way.

It had been made perhaps a week before, and when he came to a tuft of grass hung in a willow fork, Nanuk saw that the toboggan had halted and the hunter's snowshoe track went off to one side; he guessed that this was an Indian trap line and that the tuft indicated the position of a set.

He did not investigate further, for another person's traps are as sacred to an Innuit as to a Chipewyan.

He was interested to see that the trapper's tracks showed him to be wearing narrow snowshoes, such as he himself had been forced to make so painfully; and he realized that unwittingly his own snowshoes had conformed to the most practical pattern for walking through brush.

He knew he must soon meet the savage Indians whom the Innuits feared. He himself had never even seen one, for his people avoided contact with them.

He did not know how they spoke or if he would understand them, but he supposed he would be able to speak to them by signs, and he was more curious than apprehensive.

2

When he did see the Chipewyan camp, it came as no great surprise to Nanuk and less to Ahneek, for the big dog had been

1. *The Bear Presents a Broadside Shot*

2. *The Shaman*

3. Nanuk Making Arrows

4. On the Trail

5. Wolves at the Bear Carcass

6. *Nanuk Meeting the Chipewyans*

7. *Muskrat Trapping*

whining and looking about for at least an hour, and the boy easily guessed that something new was ahead.

Breaking through a thick tangle of willows set with a few shaggy spruce, the two stood for a moment looking toward a little cluster of smoke-stained lodges. The lodges were set in the lee of a grove of jack pine which topped a sandy ridge, the outspread upper limbs of the trees looking somehow grotesque against the pale sky.

Nanuk could see people moving about; smoke going up from many fires.

With Ahneek by his side, he moved slowly and deliberately forward. Suddenly, with a chorus of yapping barks, a group of lean sleigh dogs left the tents and rushed toward them, half menacingly, half in play.

Ahneek answered with a roar and ran toward them. They met halfway, the big yellow husky and the nondescript mongrels, all stopping as one in their several places.

The leader of the Indian curs finally stepped forward to within a few paces of Ahneek, stiff-legged and wary. He was as tall as the dog he faced, but less heavily built, with a gray, battle-scarred muzzle.

Ahneek turned sideways, also stiff-legged and with his bushy tail tightly curled over his haunches, his ears and mane erect, his lip curled.

Thus they stood, tense, their eyes on each other, growling deep in their shaggy throats.

Nanuk strode nearer, and several men from the camp began to approach at a jog trot.

Suddenly both dogs moved at once, silently now. In seconds the two were in the blurred rough-and-tumble of a fight, the other few looking on, ready to back the winner.

Ahneek, impeded by his pack, was almost downed by the first shock of the onslaught but recovered quickly, fighting for a hold.

Nanuk ran to the dogs, calling his own, while the Indians began to lay about them with sticks until the animals were parted. The boy seized Ahneek by his harness, which came loose, for his collar had parted where his enemy had sought to seize him by the throat but had encountered the hide instead.

The Indian dog had a torn ear, from which Ahneek's teeth would never have parted had the fight not been interrupted.

Honors even, with the odds perhaps in favor of Ahneek, the two animals stood panting but no longer enemies.

Assured that his friend was not hurt, Nanuk now looked up to find himself facing the Chipewyans.

3

Of the three, the man in the center was the older. He wore a hooded parka-coat of glazed moosehide, the sleeves heavily fringed, and the hood trimmed with wolverine fur.

Around his waist was a frayed sash in which a sheathed knife was stuck. Patched pants of faded blue cloth covered his legs to the knee, below which were moccasins with feet of tanned hide, puckered at the seams, and tops of cloth.

His companions were garbed in similar style except that they both wore hooded coats of blanket cloth, once white but now gray, and cross-striped with black and red.

All this Nanuk took in at a glance, while noticing that these men were leaner and taller than most Innuits, with faces less flat, eyes larger, and cheekbones prominent; their leanness of face was accentuated by their black shoulder-length hair.

None was armed except the man with the knife and the one at his left, who carried a small, a very small, rifle; but they all grasped the stout sticks with which they had parted the dogs.

Both parties stood and stared for a moment—the slender, well-grown youth with his pale face, and the coppery Indians, smelling of buckskin and willow smoke.

Then the center man stepped a pace forward and spoke in a series of guttural clicks. He was evidently asking a question.

And because he spoke first, Nanuk took him for the headman

of the village and politely extended his left hand, the heart-hand, as he made the only reply he could.

Touching his heart with his right forefinger, he said, "Innuit."

Whereupon the three stared again and began to talk among themselves. Then they looked again at him, their faces dark and scowling.

The chief stepped closer, and while Nanuk, his heart beginning to pound, stood straight and unflinching, the Indian lightly touched his blond, downy cheek and then pointed to the snow.

"Innuit," said the boy again.

The chief turned to the others, and they spoke among themselves again, one pointing north, another south.

Now Nanuk removed the worn piece of caribou hide which covered his shoulders and held it out to them. They gathered around with grunts of recognition, one pointing to the north again.

Then one of them spoke haltingly in another tongue with an upward inflection, and he heard the word "Eskimo" for the first time in his life. But he did not understand the speech and remained silent.

Again another spoke haltingly, repeating the word "Moonias" several times. But the boy knew no more of Cree than he did of English.

Ahneek came to his master's side, growling slightly, and the three drew back a little, for indeed the dog was large and strong. The man with the small rifle slightly raised his weapon, but dropped its muzzle again to watch while Nanuk took the pack from Ahneek's back.

When the long-haired piece of hide lay beside the caribou skin, they stared hard and put their hands over their mouths; while the one who had spoken in Cree exclaimed questioningly, *"Wha! Mishi Makwa?"* at which the boy, not understanding the meaning, but mistaking the question for one of the Innuit words connected with fire, brought from his parka the fire stick.

The Indians exclaimed again, taking the stick in their hands, turning it and smelling the charred and blackened point. One of them pointed to the boy's snowshoes and laughed, showing white teeth. Another came closer and touched the bow which hung from the boy's shoulder.

He smiled and nodded, pointing first to the little stick and then to the bow, making sawing motions with his right hand. Again the three covered their mouths, their eyes bright with interest.

4

They had all seen the little skinned squirrel which had been wrapped in the bearskin, and now they seemed to be searching for something else, things which perhaps they expected, things he would soon see for the first time such as sugar and flour. But the boy did not know what they searched for; and on an impulse he plunged his hand into his parka and brought out one of the long curved claws he treasured.

This he handed to the chief, who exclaimed and smiled and seemed pleased. He made no move to return it, but stood looking from it to the long scars on the dog's side; so Nanuk half turned to show his parka all roughly patched on its upper arm, and pointed to it. The Indians again talked among themselves, indicating in turn the boy, the dog, and the claw.

Then the chief, apparently happy with his gift, made the motion of eating, seizing an imaginary piece of meat with his teeth and making upward motions with his right hand as if to cut it away; for this is how both Indians and Innuits eat their meat.

Nanuk nodded vigorously, at which they turned and beckoned him to follow. The four, with Ahneek following close, now started toward the smoking tents.

CHAPTER FIFTEEN

1

While the questioning was going on, a little crowd of people had gathered in front of the tents, some young men and a few ancients in front. Several shawled women, full of curiosity, had left the lodges to stand, ready for flight, behind the men; their children peeped from behind their full skirts of faded print.

The little group made way as the chief approached with his entourage, the stranger in their midst. He stopped by a tepee before which a fire smoked, at which the chief's wife arose from where she had been stirring a large black pot and entered the lodge. At a word from the chief she reappeared carrying several battered tin bowls and crooked spoons, as well as a thick, round flour cake which they call bannock.

The chief indicated the steaming pot. The men squatted as Nanuk filled a bowl with meat that was of a coarse texture and very dark. He pointed at it and then looked inquiringly around.

Several words were spoken in the clicking tongue but one man said, in the other speech, *"Mooswa,"* and pointed to one side. Now the boy saw the most enormous set of antlers lying by the lodge; not long and skinny like a caribou's, but broad and shovel-like, fringed with many points of all lengths.

Could these antlers and this meat come from the animals whose deep slots he had seen? A deer, yet not a deer, for it must have been fully as large as the brown bear he had overcome.

As if guessing his thoughts, the man who spoke Cree got up, went aside to a tall willow, and began to break twigs as high as he could reach, indicating a browsing animal. Nanuk smiled and nodded in understanding and the man resumed his meal. The stew was good and they all ate heartily, their sharp knives chopping upward within a hairsbreadth of their noses.

He too ate his fill of moose meat and bannock and by the time the meal was finished Ahneek came to lie just behind him. The other dogs had followed, but as the rabble came close to the fire, women had appeared with sticks and, using harsh words, drove them off. But none cared to approach Ahneek with his high curled tail and sharp-pricked ears, as large as any wolf and just as powerful.

For their part Nanuk's hosts made no move to drive off the big yellow dog, who in his turn made no advances to any but his master; so by a tacit understanding the boy and his friend were not parted.

The Indians now produced tobacco and began to fill their pipes. There was tea also, real tea; hot tea sweet with sugar, into which the men stirred some white fat from a red pail.

The stars were coming out as the last tin cup was drained, and the chief, whose name sounded like Exkees, indicated the conical lodge, which he entered followed by the two travelers.

The chief pointed to some skin robes and, taking one, the boy chose a spot by the lodge wall and lay down. He was weary, yet he could not sleep.

The old familiar bustle of people moving about and speaking softly; the nostalgic smell of tobacco and human bodies; the whimper of a child, the crooning of its mother; all these brought back memories which came and went in his mind, fluttering like the little snowbirds of the summer barrens.

He thought of Nook, thickset and silent, of the wife of Nook who had mothered him, he thought of the long interminable stories told by the Old Ones. And when a drum was thumped softly in a neighboring lodge, he thought of the Shaman's quavering voice as he sang of the spirit world, and his heart became homesick within him.

But not empty. . . . Because since that day when he had felt he became a man, his faith had stood the test and never again would he be completely empty.

2

Gradually the women and children got used to the tall, silent youth who spoke by signs.

All the children wanted him to make them fire sticks and little bows; and it was they who taught him his first words of the Dene tongue, laughing at his attempts to master the clicking gutturals. He learned fast, for children are patient teachers, and though he never got beyond a halting and broken speech, he learned enough for everyday purposes.

No one bothered Ahneek, who had been well camp-trained and could be trusted to keep his nose out of pots and caches; and after the tangle-haired little ones made friends with him, even the women lost their fear of the yellow husky.

Nanuk's stay with the Chipewyans opened his eyes to many things and especially to the fallacy of the Innuits' belief that they were savage and cruel, for they showed nothing of this, and happily included him in their various activities.

He went on a moose hunt with a party of them and thrilled at the sight of a great bull which they brought down with their rifles. Its antlers were a disappointment, since at this season they were no more than two furry bumps on its forehead; the growing replacement for the wide rack the beast had shed earlier.

He felt the bulbous nose and rubbery lip, which he was later to taste as a delicacy.

On this trip he found why the Indian dogs were hitched in single file to the toboggans which took the meat to camp, winding this way and that between the trees and bumping over fallen logs; for he saw that the fan-style hitch of the Innuit would allow no room to maneuver in such circumstances.

In the camp he saw many strange pieces of equipment which the Indians, pointing east, let him know had come from the white man's store at a place they called Brochet. They spoke often of the whites and their ways. Nanuk listened, trying to understand, especially when they looked at his red hair and laughed.

There were cooking pots of various kinds, one being shallow with a long handle. In this the women sometimes cooked meat, but more often the round flour cakes to which they added dried berries and grease from the red tin pail.

They had many rifles, some big, some small.

The small ones were used for killing birds and something else, something that swam in the water but did not fly, so they were not ducks; and he was soon to know them.

3

Just behind the camp was a large lake and here the Indians fished. They pushed their nets under the ice with a long spruce pole, starting them from a hole they cut in the ice, and when the pole had gone full length, one of their own clever dogs scratched and barked where its far end lay invisible under the snow and ice. Here a man used his ice pick and, finding the end of the pole, pushed it along again. This they repeated till a long net hung in the water below the ice. Long strings were attached to each end of the net; these strings were left coiled on the ice and when the men went next morning the net was pulled by the string at one end, the fish removed from the mesh—which held them by the gills —and the net reset by drawing it back with the other string.

At this season the catch was not great, but it was a welcome change for Nanuk to eat humpbacked whitefish and lake trout, as pink as the salmon of the Innuits.

But when a woman lit a fire with a little stick, not so long as her finger and with a red head, he jumped back, for it looked like magic. Then she showed him some in a tin box, and by signs bade him take one and draw it across a piece of rough canvas. It flared, and he stood staring at the little flame till it consumed the stick and scorched his fingers, whereat he dropped the charred thing and laughed.

Indeed these people neither looked nor acted like devils at all, but people; people not unlike—except in features—the Innuit. More like them in most things than he himself was. . . .

Almost every evening one or other of the men would start to thump a skin drum and sing, while the others smoked and conversed gravely, the firelight ruddy on their faces, pools of shadow coming and going below their cheekbones.

CHAPTER SIXTEEN

1

Daily the light grew, daily the sun rose a little higher and his rays became a little warmer.

Nanuk was still puzzled as to why, having started his journey before the winter solstice, he had not been obliged to put up with those weeks of total darkness he had known each winter from childhood. He had gone toward the light, and the light had not failed him!

The thought filled him with awe and he thought, Could it be that the sun is the Great Spirit of good? Is that why the closer you get to it the bigger the trees, the more numerous the game? Then what greater wonders would he be destined to see as his journey took him farther and farther into the light?

He felt restless, anxious to be gone, but his Indian friends said, "Wait, the moon of storms is upon us, wait till the wild goose flies overhead."

2

And there came a day when his hosts beckoned him to come, and he followed. Each hunter had a bag of traps over his shoulder and several had small rifles.

They had walked barely two miles along the north shore of the lake when they came to a large bed of reeds and cattails surrounded by hard-packed drifts. In the center of the wide marsh were several small lakes, or rather ponds, connected one to the other by a small creek which wound about as if it were lost.

The ponds were thawing at the edges and there was some water on the ice itself, and as Exkees and the boy stepped from the reeds onto the frozen surface of the nearest, the chief pointed to a number of dark mounds of half-rotten vegetation which stood like little three-foot tepees on the lake.

The other Indians had already separated, each making his own way, till they were scattered out on the ice of the ponds and along the rotting shore line.

Nanuk followed Exkees, who walked deliberately to the nearest mound, chopped through the wall with a hand ax, and, setting the pan of a trap, placed it carefully within at the full length of his arm.

He indicated to the boy that these were the lodges of small animals whose skins they would sell at the store, and he pointed east again. Nanuk could not follow every word but he knew trapping, and nodded to show he understood.

While he spoke, the chief drew the soggy water reeds and bits of broken rush back into place, patting them well down so that the water below the muskrat house would not freeze, and then rose from his knees to set off for the next mound.

3

The Chipewyans finished their muskrat trapping in two weeks, during which Nanuk proved himself useful, for he was an expert skinner and could stretch a pelt as well as any.

He had been shown how to cut the white spot from the furry animal's tail and, after collecting these, to take them to the pond's edge and commit them to the water.

They tried to explain to him why this had to be done, the Cree-speaker saying, *"Kitche-Manitou,"* and pointing to the sky; from which the boy surmised that the man referred to some Good Spirit who even cared for the animals.

All the pitiful little skinned bodies were hung on the meat racks to smoke-dry; and he found the fresh ones extremely good and tasty.

The muskratting was better than usual this year, and even when the ice became too rotten and most of the lodges flooded, the Indians picked off many more of the animals with the small rifles which the Cree-speaker called *pahao paskissikun*. Most of the muskrats killed in this way were taken when swimming in open water or when feeding on little mounds of cattails and marsh grass at the water's edge.

For this bountiful harvest the little band credited the presence of the Innuit, and the chief loudly boasted of his good sense in treating the boy well, for, said he, "In the long ago they were enemies to be killed at once, yet how does one know a dead man? Truly, it is good to think twice and not shoot at shadows like a miserable Dog-Rib. And moreover, a young man who has killed the big bear of the barrens was not one to be trifled with, for the spirit of the creature was bound to be strong in him. It is good." And Exkees touched the curved claw he wore at his throat.

Nanuk did not hear that speech, for he had been behind the tents watching the chief's wife dressing a moose hide. This was laced to a pole frame, and the woman was removing the hair with long sweeps of her scraping tool, after the manner of the Innuits, except that in place of the familiar bone scraper she had a semi-circular steel blade inserted in the end of her wooden stick; another gift of the mysterious white men.

In a few days the hide was cured and smoked to a nice brownish-yellow color, and the chief's wife made him a fine pair of moccasins to replace his tattered boots of sealskin.

4

It was soon made clear to the boy that now the muskrat pelts were cured and baled up with the winter catch of lynx, fox, and ermine, the whole camp would move to a place the Cree-speaker called Brochet. This place was many miles to the east, and was also the place of the Company, which the boy took to be another name for store.

But he did not want to go east. These kind people were not his people and the south called strongly to him again. He knew the urge had been dulled by good food and company and he had lingered too long, as the homeward-bound hunter lingers too long when fur is plentiful.

The ice was still strong on the many creeks which meandered across the land, connecting a maze of small and large lakes all leading from southwest to northeast, and all these would have to be crossed. Since the Chipcwyans had apparently left their canoes farther east, they had to set out while traveling by foot and toboggan was still possible.

There came a morning of warm sunshine and blue sky across which the first early skeins of geese and cranes began to pass, their necks stretched to the north, the gabbling of the geese mingling with the metallic grating calls of the cranes. Then came a wedge of great white swans, their fluting calls adding a softer note to the wild clamor.

Nanuk followed the winging hosts with his eyes, his face uplifted, calling silently on the bird spirits to tell Nook and the wife of Nook that all was well with him.

5

Soon the skin lodges came down, and with a hurry and a bustle and the laughing of children everything was lashed to the toboggans and the cringing dogs were harnessed and hitched. The whips cracked, the cries of "Mush!" echoed among the trees and the whole company started off in single file, Exkees in the lead.

The place of tents would know the Dene no more that summer. At the margin of Reindeer Lake the toboggans would be cached and they would camp till the ice went out. Then the canoes would be taken from their pole stands among the brush, and the families would paddle across to Brochet with their fur catch, to loaf

and trade and make their short summer trips along the water-
ways; until with the early snows of winter they would turn their
dogs' noses once more to their hunting grounds, as they had done
year after year.

At the end of the first day's travel they set up camp beside
a small stream, and it was during that night that the boy made his
decision. He must go south, not east.

6

In the morning he told the Chipewyans of his wish, but they
were not pleased to see him go.

The chief tried all his powers of persuasion, while his daughter,
a girl of about the boy's own age, peeped coyly out from her father's lodge. Exkees, seeing this, suggested that perhaps Nanuk
wished to find a wife—but why go farther? Were not the daughters
of the Dene as beautiful, as strong, and as useful as the daughters
of strange people to the south?

And what is more, since Nanuk could now converse at least a
little in their tongue, would it not be better to stay? For is it not
a weary thing to learn new words and new speech?

Was not he, Nanuk, now adopted into their band, was he not
as a son? Had he been ill used? If so he had but to speak. . . .

Nanuk had not been unaware of the girl they called Xhitsoo.
He had noticed that her eyes were large and soft as a caribou
fawn's, her hands small and exquisite. He knew they were useful
too, for he had followed their deft movements as she stitched the
moccasins of golden moosehide he now wore; he had noticed
that her teeth were as white as a ptarmigan feather when she bit
her thread, while working at the gay beadwork which adorned
them. He had felt much drawn to her, and thoughts had run hotly
through him at such times, disturbing him, blotting out the real
purpose of his quest.

Yet she was not of his people, and perhaps the spirit within
him would later war with her spirit.

He realized, with something of a shock, that he had looked at her overmuch, and perhaps that was why he had tarried so long

The chief was not smiling now, following the boy's long silence, and as for Xhitsoo, she had withdrawn her face from the tent flap.

With a sudden impulse to bring the matter to an end, Nanuk reached into his parka and, feeling for the seven bear claws, detached one and brought out the remaining six.

These he held out to the chief, and was rewarded by seeing his face relax into a smile.

Exkees took the polished claws—within which would surely be a part of the spirit of the bear—gazed at them, and spoke again: "It is well then, Innuit." Pointing to the south, he added, "There lies your way. Follow across the small creeks to a river. Follow that and you will come to a camp of the whites. Go in peace," and the chief turned on his heel.

The boy's own dog carried his goods and now stood by his side. As Nanuk turned about, so did Ahneek, and the two once more set their faces a little to the right of the risen sun.

They looked back once only, from a low rise nearly half a mile from the camp, and Nanuk saw his friends for the last time. They were following the loaded toboggans in single file, disappearing behind clumps of bush, only to reappear as tiny moving specks which soon dwindled to nothing.

He had waved at first sight of them, but could not be sure that an arm was raised in return or only to ply a dog whip. Ahneek whined a little, for he had taken a liking to a small brindled bitch. Turning again, Nanuk spoke to the dog, and together they resumed their march.

CHAPTER SEVENTEEN

1

Nanuk had no further use for snowshoes now and had left his crooked, patched ones at the camp; first removing the mesh and straightening the cross-strips, which he tied in a bundle at his waist. He wondered if he needed his fire drill, for he had acquired a tinderbox, an old one not needed by its previous owner, who now had a fine new waterproof matchbox.

But the boy had not entirely trusted the new fire maker, and before leaving camp had struck sparks from it to ignite some moss. Only after several clumsy attempts had he been able to succeed, so he decided to keep his more primitive tool.

He felt stronger and more able than ever. The rest and food had fully restored him and the two made a long march that day over ground soggy with melting snow in the open, yet still holding deep drifts at the edge of the timber, so that they zigzagged in search of the best footing.

His new moccasins soon became wet, but he had packed his footwear with moose hair, and as long as he kept walking his feet were warm. He found that at each camp he would have to dry his moccasins and rub his feet well, as he had seen the Indians do.

Now a few forest birds began to appear. He saw several large hawks wheeling in the sky. They were obviously much later nesters than the horned owls whose young he now saw sitting solemn and wide-eyed on their flattened stick nests, their bodies coated with down, yet already as large as those of their savage-looking parents.

2

Waking next morning with the cool scent of the spruce in his nostrils, the boy saw a tiny bird swaying at the tip of one of these trees, singing in such loud and clear notes that he smiled. The tiny bird had a white circle round its eye, and when it flew to the ground Nanuk could see a narrow patch of ruby red on its crown. Another small bird crept headfirst down a gnarled tree trunk crying "me-me," and he thought it very fine with its reddish breast.

And in one wide opening he spied a mass of white, like a late snowbank, which suddenly erupted into a mass of spring snowbirds, wheeling and twittering, and he knew them, for did not these little songsters nest in hundreds, back there where the arctic hares patter and the ptarmigan call? Now he knew where they disappeared in winter—like him, toward the sun.

Life and movement and subtle smells were all around. The willow bark blushed red with sap, the poplar buds were fat with sticky balm, though it would be weeks before they opened, and everywhere the snow crust, wet by day and sparkling with granulations at dawn, settled lower in the heavy brush and in the lee of the big trees.

3

Nanuk had brought some dried muskrat bodies, a strip of moose meat, and two frozen whitefish with him. He had fed one fish to Ahneek the night before and now decided to cook the other for his breakfast, as it was getting soft and dark.

Toward noon he crossed a large muskeg in the center of which was a snow-free drumlin or low hump. On this a number of the brown grouse he had seen before were hopping and dancing, clucking and cooing. He left Ahneek and crawled toward them, under cover of some light brush. The first bird he shot with an arrow fluttered and lay still, and the birds closest to it flew, but the rest paid little heed except to pause and raise their heads, watching those on the wing rather than the hunter; and he was able to secure another before the whole company left with a dry drumming of wings and crossed the muskeg to the safety of the woods.

With these additions to his larder the boy resumed his journey.

4

Next day he came to a lake with many arms. This he crossed on the southwest arm, wading through water for perhaps half a dozen strides where the shore line lay half melted. From the far end of this arm a small river flowed; and he knew he had passed over a height of land, for, coming to an unfrozen rapid, he saw that the water was hurrying south as if leading him on, and he felt much cheered, for surely the land of light could not be far now.

This seemed to offer an easy route, but after one day of following its crooked course, often taking to the bank to avoid rapids, he wearied of it and struck across country straight south again.

In two or three days he found himself in a large swamp so beset with rushes and cattails that he could see little, so he swung to the right for a few miles to the nearest open ground and then left again; which brought him to a river, whether the continuation of the one he had followed or another he did not know. This river, or rather creek, for it was not wide, appeared to run fairly straight in the way he wished to go, and since its banks were heavily wooded he again took to the ice rather than struggle through the brush. And so he walked all day between low banks of willow and poplar backed by tall spruce.

5

Nanuk and Ahneek between them had eaten the birds, and the moose meat was almost finished. He would have to find game or fish soon, and decided to save the rest of the meat for emergency. The Indians had told him that within two weeks the fat sucker-mouthed fish would be running in the small creeks, and one of them had given him a three-pronged fish spear, a thing he knew how to use. He carried in his parka the metal head only, for there would be time enough to whittle a wooden shaft when the fish began to move into shallow water, and it was foolish to carry extra weight.

It was starting to get colder when he camped for the night. For the last hour the crystallized surface of the ice had been crunching noisily under his feet, telling him it was freezing hard.

Ahneek began to limp a little, for his feet were getting sore.

By the time their fire was going it came on to snow from the north in the big, wet flakes so common at that time of year. At first they melted as they fell, but soon began to gather on the ground and on the bushes. They fell spitting into his fire, which burned sullenly, its smoke hardly rising but drifting close to the ground to form a fog about him.

The boy was tired and his feet were wet, so he took off his footgear and set them to dry, rubbing his chilled feet with the dry grass which grew in clumps among the willows. He was in a sort of meadow where the creek widened, and there was a heavy growth of marsh grass growing in tussocks which were free of snow except at their base.

Before eating, the boy entered the wet willows to follow up a track on the old snow that looked like the track of one of the arctic hares he remembered. At the Chipewyan camp he had asked, by signs, if there were rabbits in this country; and they had showed him soft and silvery rabbit-skin robes, and explained as best they could that sometimes there were many, but that about two years ago they had begun to succumb to the rabbit sickness, and all through the past winter there had been none. But the Chipewyan had been told that a few were being seen again farther to the south.

The boy felt sure this track had been made by one, and as he penetrated farther into the willows in the half-light, he came upon more tracks, as well as some little berry-like pellets he recognized.

Accordingly he took a few lengths of sinew from his waist and set three snares at what he judged would be the right height, each of them hanging in twigs just above well-used trails.

This done, he returned to camp as darkness fell. He and the big dog shared the last muskrat and turned in under a rough brush shelter which Nanuk had lined with the dry tussock grass.

They tried to sleep, but both felt cold and damp as they had not done in the previous bitter weather.

6

The day broke slowly and dimly after a miserable night. Wet snow lay quite deep everywhere, and it had sifted through the shelter onto both boy and dog. The bushes hung downcurved with its weight, the tips of their limbs touching the ground. Somehow Nanuk got a fire going, using a strip of birch bark he had torn from a tree in passing the previous day and had kept dry in his parka.

Once he had a good blaze he went to his snares, pushing aside the drooping willows, which showered him with wet snow.

Two snares were empty but the third was pulled tight behind the head of a snowshoe rabbit. But all that was left of him were the shoulders and front legs, for the rest had been eaten by some night prowler, probably a mink. Disappointed, the boy returned to the fire and broiled what the mink had left him. He determined to keep a sharp lookout for more rabbit tracks.

The new snow made the ice better going for Ahneek, but worse for the boy, for it slid under his feet.

He saw no more rabbit sign, and put this down to the snow still falling and covering any new tracks at once; but in truth those he had encountered represented only a small, isolated colony just beginning to increase, such had been the severity of the cyclical plague and the keen competition among those predatory birds and animals which depended so much on the little furry beasts for their own existence.

The snow began to fall thicker and thicker, clinging to his eyelids, gathering on Ahneek till he looked like a woolly sheep, blotting out the shore-line timber barely thirty feet to either side.

Nanuk raised a mitted hand to brush the snow from his eyes when, suddenly, he stepped off into nothing, gasping and struggling in a current that whirled him among rocks and broken ice, a current that roared loud enough in his ears now, yet whose warning sound he had not heard in time, muffled as it had been by the heavy snowfall.

Ahneek too was swimming and caught his master by the scruff of his parka, making desperately for the shore, but on reaching the high bank, found himself impeded by a large block of ice he could not surmount with the weight on his jaws.

Slowly the current overcame the big dog's efforts and began to drag the two downstream, bumping them between the spume-covered rocks. Several times the boy's head went under, for he was heavy by reason of water beneath his parka. In the end Ahneek lost his hold.

Nanuk tried to swim, but his feet went down and there was no room for his arms amid the floating, hurrying ice.

He thought, in a queer detached way, that he must be close to the creek's mouth—where it must flow into a lake. There was often a rapid at such a place and he thought that tomorrow or the next day the whole creek would be a mass of moving ice, and he would have to take to the shore.

With that thought his head struck something and his mind went blank.

7

He came to among some willows on the riverbank. He was lying on a portage trail, marked by a tall spruce lobstick. He must have passed the marker for the other end of the portage without seeing it for the snow. It would have warned him of a rapid ahead, for he had learned the signs of canoe routes which were used in summer by the tribes.

The snow had stopped apart from a few desultory flakes. He was unutterably weary and shivering with cold. He looked for Ahneek but saw instead a dark face bending over him and heard the Chipewyan speech from close by. He could smell smoke and knew there was a fire. Another Indian was approaching with his arms full of spruce boughs.

Nanuk felt the darkness coming over him again and fell back, but he felt many hands seize him, heard many voices in guttural talk, and realized he was being stripped naked.

He felt the heat from the fire on one side and then a heavy robe was thrown over him and he drifted off, but this time into an uneasy sleep in which he called for Ahneek.

The next thing he knew a warm tongue was caressing his cheek and water was dripping upon him. He opened his eyes to see his dog standing over him, wet and shivering. Next, someone came with hot broth, someone who lifted his head and put the bowl to his lips. It was fish soup and he thought, "Well, the suckers must be running now." The liquid warmed his stomach and he felt it crawl to his very toes.

Nanuk sighed, turned on his side, and slept; but this time there were no dreams.

CHAPTER EIGHTEEN

1

The little Chipewyan nurses' aide turned quickly toward the bed.

Her patient, the strange white youth who could not speak English, was sitting up and staring around him. Pneumonia had left him haggard and pitifully weak.

Where was he? What was he lying on, so far from the ground? What were the bars behind his head, and what was that bottle thing with the long tube hanging from it?

It must be a trap, he thought, and started to get off the unfamiliar bed; but the aide took him by the feet and lifted his legs back.

He croaked something in Innuit and she replied in the Dene. She told him he was in the big white man's lodge at a place called Lac La Ronge; that a party of her people, camping at Mink Rapids, had taken him to Sandfly Lake, and that the yellow-stripe there had sent him here by plane.

That had been three days before. His chest, she explained, and put a brown hand on her own bosom, coughing. The white Shaman would make him well.

He understood the general drift of what she said and nodded. Then he raised his eyes to hers with a question in them. "Ahneek?" he said, in a voice he did not recognize as his own, which seemed to come from far away.

The aide shook her head. He tried again, stumbling over the word for dog. She smiled again and pointed out of the window where Ahneek lay in the spring sun, lonely and still.

The girl stepped into the hall and called a name, and a red-headed orderly entered. He looked irritated and his left hand was bandaged. In English, the aide said, "Do you mind to watch my patient a liddle wile? Don' let him get out of bed, eh?" and disappeared.

The orderly went to the window with hardly a glance at Nanuk. He watched the little aide go to Ahneek, who turned his head and pricked his ears toward her. She spoke softly in her own tongue, smiling and extending her hand. Ahneek rose, wagging his curly tail, touched her hand, and as she turned so did he, and the girl and the big dog began to mount the front steps.

The orderly drew back with a disgusted look on his face, muttering, "Wet-nursing damn Indians and stinking dogs—what a life!" He looked at his bandaged hand. "Got one good kick at the beggar, anyway. Wish he'd bite that uppity little nichie aide."

Just then the girl entered, the dog at her side, and the orderly eased out, keeping wide of Ahneek.

Ahneek bounded to the bedside and ecstatically greeted his master.

2

Nanuk did not know it, but the doctor had left orders that the husky be left strictly alone, after Pete the orderly had tried to tie him up at the back of the building. Thereafter the dog had taken up a position on the little patch of grass in front, ignoring man and beast. No town dog had dared to approach too close, and as to those people who sought to touch him, they soon saw something in the dog's appearance which made them hesitate and pass on.

Only the little aide, who knew dog language, was able to go right up to him with his evening bone, and on those occasions he would get to his feet like a gentleman and touch his nose to her hand—which had a flavor of Nanuk—before taking his supper gently from her.

Nor did the boy know a thing about hospital regulations or he would have realized what a great concession Dr. Summers had made in giving orders that when Nanuk's fever broke his companion should be brought in. "The lad knows no one," he had said, "and seems to speak only Eskimo and a bit of Chip. He will be frightened when he wakes, but the dog will calm him. It's just a lucky thing that young Ballentyne put the dog on the plane with him. According to the Indians, it was he who dragged the lad ashore. They said the dog wouldn't leave him and none of them wanted to lose an arm—nor young Ballentyne either, I dare say.

"Now listen, Madeline," he had concluded, turning to the aide, "you're not to leave the patient, see? You can put in the time knitting if you like, but don't leave him alone. Come night, get Peter the orderly to relieve you. That boy's apt to throw himself out of bed, and we don't want that—speak to him when you can, see? Try to explain where he is, make him feel at home—got it?" And the little aide had smiled and nodded.

3

It was three days before that the Indians from Mink Rapids had taken Nanuk to Sandfly Lake in a blanket and delivered him to Constable Ballentyne of the R.C.M.P., who was to them not only the law but the government.

Just before the Indians arrived, the spring packet had come in by plane from Brochet to be forwarded to Prince Albert, and with it a note from Corporal Fielding reporting the rumor of a young white man who could not speak English, who had been in old Exkees' camp at Wolverine Lake; but no one knew his proper name or where he came from. The note ended, "copies enclosed to all detachments, P.A. Division, R.C.M.P."

Constable Ballentyne at Sandfly Lake had sat long at his desk that night, punching his typewriter keys by the "hunt and peck" method. His finished report to the superintendent read something like this, omitting the preliminaries:

(1) About noon of April 22, 1945, Beaver Tail and members of his band, Johnny, Isadore, Old Fox and Atanuk

(Chipewyans), arrived from Mink Rapids, approximately twenty-seven miles northeast this point, bringing an almost unconscious man, well wrapped, together with his clothing, and with a large yellow husky dog, evidently the victim's property.

(2) Isadore's statement (in English) was to the effect that the previous day, April 21, the band was preparing to move camp to Sucker Lake and had arrived at Mink Rapids for noon meal. While they were cooking, a large husky dog had approached from the willows. The dog was soaking wet. Isadore then went toward the dog, which turned back into the brush of the riverbank. Following the dog, Isadore came upon the body of what he thought was a dead man.

He called for Atanuk and the two lifted the body and brought it to camp, only to find that it was not a grown man, but a youth of about seventeen. They also discovered that he still lived. They therefore stripped him of his wet clothes and gave what aid they could. The victim came to for a few minutes and then relapsed into unconsciousness or sleep, they did not know which.

(3) Reconstructing the accident, they think that the youth had been traveling south and had encountered the rapid unexpectedly, owing to very heavy snowfall at the time. He had evidently been swept downstream to the lower portage trail, suffering injury from rocks or ice on the way.

Apparently the dog had dragged him up the bank, as was shown by tracks in the new snow, and ragged tears about the man's parka hood, evidently made by the dog's teeth.

(4) They accordingly kept him in camp overnight, but as he was still breathing next day (April 22), they made a litter and between the five of them (named in paragraph 1) brought the victim to my detachment.

(5) *Action taken.* Since the plane from Brochet was still here, having first contacted the Senior Medical Officer, La Ronge, I persuaded the pilot to take the victim to St. Paul's

Anglican Hospital at Lac La Ronge, from where the pilot can return Brochet.

I also sent the husky dog, who understands no English, but the Chipewyans warned he might be vicious if attempts were made to part him from the young man; also the victim's parcel of belongings. I consider the dog might be a clue to victim's identity.

(6) *Reason for action.* The following description of victim and list of possessions leads to my belief that the victim is neither Indian nor Métis, but of pure white blood. That he has lived among the Eskimos exclusively until the last few months. That it will aid further investigation to have him at La Ronge, which is not so isolated as this detachment, also bearing in mind he could be more promptly cared for, as the plane was available, since it might be days before a doctor could reach Sandfly Lake.

Followed a description of the victim:

Name—Not known.

Height—Five feet eight inches, slim.

Age—16–18 years. Beard beginning to show.

Colouring—Fair. Blue eyes, red hair. Freckles.

Marks—White scars (old) on arms and lower legs. Large bruise on back of head. Healed wound on muscles of left forearm, evidently not attended by doctor, as deeply pitted as with animal teeth.

General state—Victim in state of shock. Pneumonia feared as he talked in apparent delirium.

Speech—Apparently Eskimo, with a few words of Chipewyan. One Cree word—*mooswa*. No English.

Possessions—All these are old and badly worn except *Chipewyan-style moccasins,* recently made.

Fire drill and bow, Eskimo style. Also tinderbox apparently obtained from Chipewyans, since marked in syllabic characters, with non-Eskimo name.

Case knife, similar to those traded to Eskimos for seal-skinning.

One bear claw in parka. Too large for black bear, but could be polar bear or more likely barren-land bear from few dark hairs still adhering.

A few strands sinew, look like barren-land caribou, and small piece of untanned hide of same.

A ragged length of what might have been a woolen blanket, with two letters interwoven which read V.Y. in faded blue. Blanket is not Hudson's Bay cloth but appears to be camel hair. Evidently of white make.

Pack carried by dog, made of a rolled-up piece of same type of bear as above, containing a few scraps of dried meat. Fastened to animal by rawhide thongs.

Dog. A typical large Eskimo husky, with sore feet and scarred flanks, but otherwise in good shape. Very stand-offish and perhaps dangerous to strangers, but obviously devoted to victim. Since latter constantly repeated the word "Ahneek," I tried it on the dog, who responded, so I take it that the victim called the dog by this Eskimo name, which I believe means "friend."

Recommendations.

I believe the victim will be able to give an account of himself in the Eskimo speech, and therefore respectfully suggest an Eskimo-speaking white or Indian be sent to La Ronge to interview him.

References.

Please refer to report from Corporal Fielding at Brochet dated April 20, 1945. There would seem to be a connection here.

      Copies to: Corporal Fielding, Brochet.
               R.C.M.P., Lac La Ronge.
               Senior Medical Officer, St. Paul's Hospital,
                         Lac La Ronge.

Constable Ballentyne signed the report, licked and stamped the envelope, dropped it into the "out" tray for the next plane, yawned, and went to bed.

CHAPTER NINETEEN

1

Superintendent Young leaned back, filled his pipe, locked his hands behind his head, and gazed at the ceiling, toward which the blue smoke was curling and eddying.

It was sixteen lonely years since he had lost Elspeth, his wife. Sixteen years in which he had thrown himself into his work with a sort of savage fervor for the sake of forgetfulness. The years had taken their toll even as they had led from promotion to promotion. He had tried to get overseas, but the assistant commissioner had made it very plain that he could serve his country better in the force.

His mind went back to his first northern posting, to the little drab detachment at Coronation. How bleak it had been without her, since the plane she had been coming home on was lost in the desolation of the treeless, soggy tundra; somewhere between the Mackenzie River and Hudson's Bay.

He had loved the country—the great spaces, the sense of freedom; the knowledge that he, a lone constable of the mounted police, was helping to roll back the map of Canada, establishing the rule of law among the almost unknown tribes. Not that the coastal bands were so much strangers to the white men; they had met Europeans long ago. They had seen Franklin's ships. They had met whalers and fur traders.

But the interior bands had been another matter. Those caribou-hunting nomads of the barrens, here today and gone tomorrow, were shy, suspicious, and not easily known.

He shifted restlessly and relit his pipe, which had gone cold. And he brought his mind back from its wanderings, and remembered how love had turned to cold hate for a land so secretive, so furtive, so quick to blot out forever those who trespassed on its lonely silence.

Well, he hadn't turned tail. The Old Man had offered a transfer on compassionate grounds. But he had refused. His, he felt, was the grim task of helping in the search. But as the months went by the search planes and patrols had been dispersed; and all he could do was to inquire and inquire ceaselessly on his long patrols, wearing himself to the bone, losing weight and becoming more sharp-featured and bleak of face as time went on.

He could no longer remember exactly how many patrols he had made, how many camps he had visited, but his reports, he supposed, would still be on file at Aklavik.

Every post, every Company store, every mission had been notified, but not a word or a hint had come from out that sullen, frozen desert.

2

His eyes dropped to Constable Ballentyne's report, lying loosely shuffled on his desk.

Here was a lad of sixteen who had come from nowhere. No, not nowhere; for all signs pointed to the north, to the barrens.

But the lad was white, red-haired—and freckled! He had seen Eskimo kids who looked pretty white. Even odd ones with a tinge of red in their hair.

But freckles? He had never seen such things as those on the flat faces of an Innuit—or even a part Innuit.

Elspeth had been freckled—he killed that thought. He must think clearly, analytically, like the policeman he was.

What else? The young fellow apparently spoke no English or other European language; only the Innuit tongue. How well? he wondered.

Ballentyne wouldn't know. He had only a vague smattering of

Eskimo; but he was no fool. He had a good ear or he wouldn't have mastered Chipewyan so well in a little over two years.

What of the piece of blanket the constable had so carefully described? Those initials . . .

V.Y.! His own family name was Young. Oh, damn! Then something came out of the past and nudged him. He looked at his watch.

With a word to the orderly, the superintendent donned his pea jacket, picked up his crop, and stepped across to his quarters.

Going to an old-fashioned escritoire, he fumbled about for a moment and came up with a packet of letters tied with store string.

He took out the top one, the last one, dated Edmonton, February 1929.

Opening it, he took out the folded sheets and began to glance over them. His hands trembled and he steadied them on the edge of the desk.

Yes, here it was, on the third page . . . "and Aunt Emma says his name must be Victor. It's really laughable the way she insists! I think she's afraid we'll call him Butch or Sonny or Junior or some awful name like Rett! She even wove the initials for Victor Young into that blanket she sent from Kingston. Oh, I forgot to tell you that she sent a lovely blanket—camel's hair and what not—you know how mad she is on weaving. Says it keeps her busy and helps her to *express* herself! And she'd woven those initials *right in*—so they can't be changed! I suppose after that we'll just have to call him Victor, after his grandfather. . . ."

Victor Young! V.Y.!

His mind reeled as he stumbled over to the phone. Then, "This won't do," he said aloud, and sat down to fill his pipe, concentrating on packing the tobacco neatly, striking a match with care.

Only when he had full command of himself did he pick up the instrument.

"Get me Sergeant Wilde," he said in his usual crisp voice.

"Sergeant Wilde? Can you have the plane ready by three o'clock? . . . Yes? . . . Good! I have to go to La Ronge—yes, yes. I'll see you at the office at one-thirty. Thank you."

3

In the cramped seat of the little plane the superintendent had to put his briefcase on his knees. Now he opened it and took out a sheaf of papers. He studied his notes carefully, crossing out this, adding that. He compared them with young Ballentyne's report and the note from Fielding at Brochet. Ballentyne was no fool, he thought for the second time that day. He had done his work well, and there might be a stripe for him in this.

He was laboriously trying to piece things together, but he mustn't jump to conclusions and look too far ahead, or he'd go nuts.

What if this were some half-breed boy who'd got lost? Well, working on the assumption that he had been raised by Eskimos, why—if he had become lost—would he have come south all that weary seven hundred miles or more? If he had stayed where he was, surely his people would have found him?

And from where would he—or his people—have stolen or picked up that blanket?

Had he been attacked by a bear and left for dead? With only a bitten arm?

He reread what the report said about the scars on the lad and on the dog, the bear claw and the piece of grizzly hide.

If the boy had seemed so badly wounded as to be left, who or what had resuscitated him? Who had killed the bear? If it was the Innuits, surely they would have taken all of the valuable hide —and all the claws. They were worth a good deal in trade.

No. It didn't matter how he turned it, he always made two and two equal three or five, never four—unless . . .

He closed his briefcase and looked down over the now greening bush country: the tamaracks in the dun swamps faintly emerald, the poplars misty with pearly catkins, the dark spears of the spruce pointing to the sky, rank on rank.

Whiteswan Lake was a blue ribbon to the east; Trout Lake,

Mecymot Lake and its winding river below him; to the north the island-dotted expanse of Lac La Ronge, and coming ever closer as they lost altitude, the white walls and red roof of the Anglican hospital.

CHAPTER TWENTY

1

The superintendent was facing Dr. Summers over a cup of coffee.

"Well, Doctor," he said at last, "what do you think? I want to see this lad, but not till I hear what you have to say. What I have told you is at present in confidence. So far, it's just a guess. And I don't want to build on it; you understand? I'd rather treat it as a straight police case. I speak Eskimo like a native, you know, or I might have sent someone else."

The doctor stubbed out his cigarette and looked at the wall. "I can tell you one thing," he said, "the boy is pure white. For another thing, he's not shamming. He doesn't know a word of English.

"Also, I am firmly convinced he was brought up in the wilds by natives—whether Eskimos or Indians, it's up to you to find out, for I know neither language. But it's perfectly obvious that he never even saw a bed—I mean a proper bedstead—until he came here. He was too frightened of it!"

"Er—about being brought up by natives?" queried the superintendent. "How do you know?"

"Oh yes—sorry. The fellow's legs are a mass of small scars. Looks as if he'd been playing with dogs—or some other animals." He glanced quizzically at the policeman. "When he was small, of course," added the doctor. "Anyway, they are tooth marks of some sort. I've seen something like it before—not so many, though—and I don't know to what extent natives allow their kids to rough-and-tumble with dogs. The scars are bigger than one would expect from small pups. . . ."

"Well, what about this husky that's with the lad—and by the way, Doctor, it was a brain wave of yours to allow his pal to stay near him—but would that dog have made those scars?"

"I think not," was the reply. "The fellow is just as near as dammit to sixteen or even seventeen; whiskers showing up and all that. And the dog can't be that old. His teeth are sound, and he's not lazy like an old beast. Even ten is pretty old for a dog in these parts.

"No, I don't think it was this dog. For one thing, by the look of them, those scars have been on him since he was a crawler, I'd say. Almost makes one think of the sort of thing one's heard of in India. . . ."

The doctor lit another cigarette. "Anything else?"

"Yes—what about that wounded arm?"

"Animal of some kind. It only dates from a few months past. I'd say a wolf or a bear. Strongly points to bear, because if the same animal tackled the dog, it's been clawed on the flanks; and wolves don't have sharp claws, do they? It would take a big wolf, too, to take a man's whole arm in his mouth and mark it up like that. Could be some connection with the bear hide—and the claw."

"Did you see the piece of blanket mentioned in this report?" asked the superintendent as he looked up from his notes.

"Oh sure. I've looked over his clothes and had them fumigated for safety's sake. Looks like a bit of crib blanket to me. Made of some kind of wool we don't see in this part of the country.

"Seems it was his 'medicine,' as they say. He doesn't want to part with it. Holds it a lot, like . . . well, you've seen a little kid dragging something around? A teddy bear or—a piece of rag or cloth? Sort of a security thing. Takes the place of mother and all that stuff."

"Okay. Thanks." The policeman rose. "I'm ready to see him now."

2

As the superintendent entered the private ward, a big yellow dog rose from beside the bed and advanced on stiff legs. He spoke a word in Eskimo and the husky settled down again.

The boy was sitting up in bed staring at him with wide blue eyes. The aide rose from her chair, rolled up her knitting, and moved toward the door.

"Please stay, Sister," said the superintendent.

Smiling, pleased at being addressed as Sister, she sat down again and began to ply her needles.

Nanuk was thin and pale, and his freckles were more noticeable than usual. They stood out sharply on the skin stretched tightly over his cheekbones, the skin now white with the pallor of illness, its outdoor color gone.

The tall man gripped the foot of the bed with his hands till the knuckles whitened. Controlling himself, he smiled. The boy smiled back.

My God! Was this Elspeth looking at him? But no, he must push that back. He mustn't hurt himself. All redheads had a similar look—they were a type.

"Do you like this place?" the policeman asked in Eskimo, hardly knowing how to begin—he who had questioned hundreds. "Are you afraid here?" he added.

"No," replied Nanuk in the same language. "I am not afraid. The savage girl"—he indicated the aide—"she brings me good food. Some I do not like—I would like more meat. I know a little of her speech, and she tells me I shall soon have more. That is good. An Innuit must have fat meat, not white things.

"I have not spoken my speech here before. It is good to speak it again. Are you another white *angakok* like the one who pricks me sometimes and laughs?"

"No, I am not a shaman," and the superintendent came around the bed to stand by the invalid's shoulder.

Nanuk looked him up and down, gazing long at the badges which looked like the heads of musk oxen. Then he stretched out a hand and touched the stripe on the police breeches. He twiddled it between finger and thumb.

"No," he said, "for I perceive that you are a yellow-leg warrior. I have heard of them. They can hang people," he added.

"And have you seen one before, or touched one?" The question came rapidly, for again he seemed to be questioning Nook, and felt again a child's hand on his leg. A child with blue eyes—but that was not uncommon among the Innuits, and the light had been bad. . . .

The boy wrinkled his brow. "I do not remember," he said. "Perhaps it was a dream."

Changing the subject, the man went on. "Do you know of a man of the Innuit called Nook?"

"Nook? Why, Nook is my—no—my man, in whose tent I lived. But that was long ago. Before ever the snow came."

"Did you get lost, then, on a hunting trip?"

"Lost, Father?" The superintendent started at the word. "Never is an Innuit lost. No, not lost, but I had to leave. The spirit said so, for I had to follow the light. They were not my people. I did not know who my people were. But now I know. They are the people who are your people, whose eyes are like the sky and their skin pale.

"That is why I left, for does the seal live with the caribou? And I am in the Sign of the Bear," he added.

"And how did you first come to the place of the tents, of Nook and his band?"

"I do not know. Perhaps I have always been there, or perhaps Nook found me. He is a mighty hunter and kills the white bears. Perhaps it was the doing of my medicine which I have always had"; and from under his pillow the boy withdrew a piece of threadbare blanket, freshly laundered but badly stained. "This is my medicine, and it bears the marks of a lodge," indicating the two woven letters; but he held them upside down and the superintendent saw what he meant. "And I have come to the lodge," added the boy. "I had to find it, for there would be my people. It is a much greater lodge than I expected, but I have heard it said that all things are greater among the yellow-legs."

"And what did your medicine say you would find in the great lodge?" pursued his questioner.

"Not my medicine, Father." Among the Innuits, the superintendent knew (as among the Indians), it was common for a young man to address a respected elder by the title of father. "It was the spirit who told me—not a bad spirit, no. It said, 'Go to the lodge of your own people. Go to the lodge of many colors and find there the man who is your father,' " and the boy gazed long at the face so close to his.

His years of training restrained the superintendent.

Not too soon, his mind told him above the clamor of his heart. He must go slow for both their sakes.

The boy's flushed face now fell back upon the pillows.

The aide rose. "De patient mus' have his med'cine now, plis," she said. She had not understood a word, but she knew her responsibility. "He will have de fever again, so plis leave if you don' mind."

The superintendent stepped back. He felt a cold nose in his hand and, looking down, saw the big husky close to his thigh.

He spoke to it and, turning, left the ward, his mind racing.

CHAPTER TWENTY-ONE

1

"So, Doctor," the superintendent concluded, "I didn't dare go further until I was absolutely *dead* sure. See what I mean?"

"Yep," grunted the doctor. "But there's still another way. Not *quite* dead sure, but it has stood the test of a court of law.

"I mean blood analysis. I took a sample from the boy this morning. Oh, he wasn't scared! He's used to the needle anyway. Only I didn't tell him what I was doing this time. Never can tell with natives—they have all sorts of notions about blood, y'know. I've a trained girl here who can make the tests. What d'you say?"

And he picked up a hypodermic needle.

The superintendent, wondering if he was dreaming, rolled up his sleeve.

"Good. We'll know in the morning," the doctor said dryly.

About to leave, the policeman turned at the door. "Your intercom working?" he asked.

"You bet. Want to use it? I'll show you." The doctor joined him. "Good girl to help you, too. Métis. You just give them a chance and a little training and you can't beat them. Come along!"

The doctor was proud of his building and his modern equipment, but even more so of the staff he had trained so patiently. He loved the north country, which he invariably spoke of as "her."

They entered a small room where a dark-haired girl sat by a thing of knobs and lights.

"Oh, Julie—take care of Superintendent Young, will you?"

The girl nodded brightly.

"Get me Aklavik if you can, please. R.C.M.P."

She twirled some knobs, and her voice sounded loud in the little room.

"La Ronge calling . . . calling. Come in, please. . . . Over!

"Hello, yes—thank you. Superintendent Young."

She handed him the earphones as she slid from the stool.

The inspector sat before he spoke. "Young this end. Reference Nook. Caribou Eskimo band, Coppermine area. Got it? Check reports, patrols back to 1929. Loss of plane carrying Mrs. Young and child, March 1929. And subsequent search patrols to 1933, with special reference to native hunter Nook. File C 16R-400, I think. Repeat, please. Over."

He heard the voice at Aklavik repeat and turn over.

"Thank you. Now, can you check the following two files? One: Any report adoption of white child by natives since 1929. Two: Any reports of natives lost since 1944 if files still open. Repeat, please. Over. . . .

"Okay. Thanks. Can you let me have this information over this station tomorrow noon? Over."

Yes, they could, and the superintendent rose.

"Thank you, Julie. Let me know when they call back tomorrow, will you? If I'm not right here, I mean."

He returned to the doctor's office.

"Just put a call in to Aklavik. Might turn something up."

"Good," exclaimed the doctor. "Now *I* want to know that you get a decent night's sleep; so take two of these in a glass of water, and to bed with you. And I don't want you mucking around here till one o'clock tomorrow, get it? If you need anything, buzz the nurse. Yes, your bed's in Ward Three. Good night!"

2

In spite of the pills, Young slept badly. He dropped off quickly enough, but his was a broken sleep.

The boy's pleading eyes kept coming between him and something. The boy's mouth would open but no words come.

Then he was at the place of tents and someone was pulling at his pant leg. Looking down, he saw it was a big dog that presently turned into a bear. It had him by the throat and he struggled and half woke. Then he was in a plane, looking down, the earth rushing toward him. Then a voice—Elspeth's voice—above the shriek of the wind, "Oh, God! Save . . ." And there she was. He tried to touch her but could not.

He had tried to count the freckles on her face but she dissolved and he saw her no more; while a faint voice called: "Aklavik calling. Come in, Victor, come in, Victor."

He woke then, sweating. He switched on the light and reached for his pipe, which he lit with unsteady hands, and lay looking at a text on the wall with the words "Behold, I make all things new."

After a few minutes of deep thought he put down his pipe and laid down, switching off the bedside lamp.

He slept heavily this time.

When he woke the spring sun was streaming in, and through the open window he could hear the birds. An aide entered with a tray.

3

At ten-thirty the superintendent rose, shaved, and began to dress. He was strangely at peace, leisurely in his movements. He looked in the glass to brush his thinning hair and noticed how gray he had become. Well, forty-five wasn't young any more. Elspeth would now be thirty-eight; but he couldn't, somehow, visualize that. . . .

A tap at the door, and the doctor entered. He had two blue forms in his hand.

His thoughts interrupted, Young turned with a start. "Well?"

"Well, Superintendent, the blood test backs up the rest. Take a look at this!"

Together they bent over the forms.

"I think that settles all doubt, eh?" the doctor said. "But take it easy—the lad's sleeping. And by the way, he's much better; he'll be out of here in a few days. That is," he smiled, "if we can find a good place for him to convalesce; something better than a hospital. But I wouldn't see him till after lunch—if you can wait that long?"

"I can wait," was the quiet answer. Now he was sure, both mind and heart were at ease. I've waited sixteen years, he thought; another hour or two won't matter.

There was no need in his mind for further proof. Nevertheless, it came.

Julie called him to the radio room just after twelve, and Aklavik reported the only two mentions of Nook was in his (then Constable Young's) report of patrol of 1932. Quote: "At camp of Caribou Eskimos seventy miles southeast Coppermine River. One Nook questioned, who seems to be chief hunter. No signs of plane seen by this band." Unquote.

And December 31, 1944, report from Constable Burkett, Coronation. Quote: "On the 27th instant, Mr. McLeod, Hudson's Bay post manager, states, quote: 'Solomon Atseek, local native, told me he had heard rumor brought by member of Bathurst Inlet seal hunters that he had been told by member of Caribou band, now in winter camp about seventy-five miles southwest of inlet, that a member of that band, son of one Nook, a hunter, had been missing for some weeks. On being questioned further, said missing man was not son of Nook, but adopted.'

"No confirmation from any natives I have questioned, and felt patrol not justified as weather bad, and there has been some sickness among the bands.

"Await instructions if any, otherwise will check on regular spring patrol before breakup." End of quote.

That was all, but it was enough. He remembered questioning Nook and almost remarking on the blue-eyed Eskimo child. What a secretive people. He wondered if they had been afraid to speak.

To think that he had been within touching distance of his own son! Why had he not turned back when his mind had been uneasy? Why do we, he thought, choose to ignore such feelings as had nagged at him that day, after he had left Nook's camp? He supposed that, for one thing, his mind had already accepted the total loss of his boy by that time, and the feeble questioning of his heart (his "hunch" if you like) had not been able to break through the barrier which kept his rational side separated from his emotions. Or, he thought wryly, kept the policeman separated from the father!

Yet how wondrous are the ways of God, he added to himself, and realized that of course he *had* known his own flesh and blood when first he entered the ward.

All that would remain now would be to try to solve the mystery of how Victor—yes, Victor, he savored the name—had come to the Innuit camp. Nook, they said, was a hunter of bears, and could that prove a clue? He would fly north next summer—take a vacation. It was coming to him, for he had not asked for leave for years. Yes, and take Victor with him. Then perhaps he would be able to give a proper burial to the boy's poor mother.

4

Victor was sitting in a chair by the window, the hospital dressing gown hanging loosely on his lean figure.

Ahneek stood by him; and at the superintendent's entrance the two turned their heads toward him.

There was a moment of silence as three pairs of eyes met.

"You are my son, Victor," said the tall man at last.

"Yes, I know," replied the boy, and Ahneek stepped forward and pressed against the father's thigh, looking from one to the other.

"How did you know?"

"Am I not one born in the sign of the great bear? How else did it come that I left the place of tents to come here? How else did I know my father to be a yellow-stripe? Have I not a powerful medicine of marks?

"I think I am an old thing, for I have much wisdom. Indeed I would have spoken before, but it is not for a son to speak first, O my father.

"The sign of the bear is very strong in my heart and the bear was before us. Yet the sign is not the spirit—it but shows the way of the spirit, I think. It brought me from the land of dark to the place of light, all on my two feet!

"I shall live with you and learn to speak the Inglis speech and learn many things; and I shall be a great *angakok,* healing all manner of troubles of the belly and of the heart and making things new.

"I have waited since dawn for you, and you will tell me of my mother, for I know she does not live now, and when I can, I shall go to Nook and the wife of Nook who took me and cared for me, that I may be forgiven for leaving them as they grow old. And the wife of Nook was barren and had no children of her own, whereby I am much in their debt.

"Now, my father, let us make haste and leave this place where there are none who understand, saving this savage woman who has been kind. She gave me this." Victor indicated a blue knitted scarf hanging on his chair. "She said that each stitch was a thought from her that I would get well. For that I felt warm toward her and gave her my bear's claw, for it has done its work.

"Oh yes, and Ahneek knew you even as I knew you. That is why he presses against you, for he perceives the same spirit in both of us.

"Come, shall we go?"

CHAPTER TWENTY-TWO

1

Superintendent Young was talking to his housekeeper.

Mrs. Gilchrist had been with him for years. She had raised a big family in her day, and now that there was a young man in the house she was happy.

". . . so I think I'll get Father Parker to tutor him. Mr. Parker tells me that time hangs heavy on his hands, and he used to be a schoolmaster before he took orders and worked in the northern missions. He knows the Innuits and their language, and he'll soon have Victor speaking English.

"The Eskimos are pretty smart people and they learn fast. I'll bet by this time next year he'll be ready for St. John's College. He'll be able to show the other fellows a lot about the outdoors —survival and all that.

"Does he like his room, d'you think?"

"Yes, sir, he likes it. I left him staring at that photo of his mother—poor soul—and I expect he's asleep now.

"I'll be glad when he learns to sit on a chair like a Christian, and use a knife and fork! Yet in other ways a better-mannered boy *I* never saw—and him brought up by them heathen people. I always say, blood will tell.

"And the dog too, he's well-mannered, though he don't know 'sick'em' and I never did like animals in the house, but I dursn't cross him anyways!

"Just look at him now! Out front there and the kids a-riding on his back!"

2

There was rejoicing in the tents of the Caribou Eskimos. The long secret was out at last, and they had received thanks and many presents and greetings from Nanuk, instead of blame.

Certainly the ways of the white man, which they had thought beyond comprehension, were not so different to their own, after all.

When the yellow-leg from Coronation had come and told them that Nanuk had found his people and his father, the camp was astonished—all but the Shaman.

It was the Shaman himself who now addressed the Innuits as they sat smoking new tobacco through the long, bright night.

"What did I say? Did I not say he was to follow the light? Did ye think it idle talk?

"I knew he had to leave, and that is why I told you not to spend overlong in search. That is why the snow spirits came to cover his tracks. Had he not passed the test of hairs, the test of the tooth? Was it not that he might be nurtured for this?

"I knew then that I spoke to fools; which is why I covered my words as a wild goose covers its eggs.

"Now my words have hatched, as I knew they would, for I am old and I am patient. What are years, say? They are but moments that pass as the caribou herd passes, leaving only imprints and dung. But the years are also for counting the time, and there is a time for this and a time for that according to the passage of years.

"It was not the time for you to speak of the child when he was small. And so I told you, for he might not have profited.

"Now is another time, the time to speak, and it is well you have spoken all to the yellow-leg who came among us yesterday, O Nook; for now that the boy has accomplished that which was required, it is greatly to his profit—and ours," he added.

"And now if I were to tell you that the youth Nanuk, suckled by a bear, nurtured by the wife of Nook, if I were to say that this young man will return—who knows when?—will be a mighty shaman, an *angakok* with dominion over bears, seeing their thoughts, a shaman curing all ills, then neither will you believe me, for these be ill days for men of wisdom, and my words will be like the rising of a fish in water—a little ripple soon forgotten.

"And the spirits have told me that by dawn there will be, beside my tent, dried fish, and some oil and the fat from a caribou's kidney.

"For it is a hard matter to commune with the spirits and make divinations for your sakes, and keep more than a thousand secrets, and the flesh on my bones is becoming stringy and lacking fat by reason of those things."

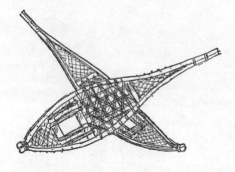